THE BLACK WIDOW

Eva

45th Class Reeva

Read with Joy

Phyll I.

Hawthorne Houts

THE BLACK WIDOW

PHYLL T.

authorHOUSE®

AuthorHouse™
1663 Liberty Drive
Bloomington, IN 47403
www.authorhouse.com
Phone: 1-800-839-8640

First published by AuthorHouse   11/02/2011

ISBN: 978-1-4670-6865-9 (sc)
ISBN: 978-1-4670-6863-5 (hc)
ISBN: 978-1-4670-6862-8 (ebk)

Library of Congress Control Number: 2011919226

Cover Illustration by: Gerrin Tramis

Printed in the United States of America

For All My Children: Fela, Kyle, Derek, Gerrin, Jordan, Christi, and Leslie—I give this gift to you for life. The treasure is yours!

For my Grand children: Marina, Kynan, Vlad, and Ashlyn— Keep your imagination and explore the adventure, it is a gift!

For Tramis: you gave me life to write.

For my close friends: you gave me time to listen to all my stories and encouraged me to write them.

And for my computer guy: Curtis, thank you so much!

PROLOGUE

THE WAY THE story goes, as the old timer tells it, sometime in the 1700s, there were pirates who lived and sailed their ships across the oceans in search of places to hide their treasure. Along the shore of our southern regions of North America where the inland coastal rivers meet were caves near the banks. The wind had a way of whistling through them and could be heard by the local people. For that reason alone they were called the Caves of Wind. There was much speculation that pirate treasure was buried in the caves. Most of that speculation came from the old timer who would tell stories of the treasure hidden by pirates, but his favorite story was about Captain Greybellow, Captain Kilo, and Zang. Of course he never left out the stories about the mighty pirate ship, *The Black Widow,* and the secret of the magic golden eggs.

He always began his story like this: Once there were two powerful captains in the English Navy, Thaddeus Greybellow and Francesco Kilo. Both were favored by the king of England. The king commissioned a voyage with Captain Kilo at the helm to search for the magic ostrich eggs from Africa that carried special powers and bring them to England. Now, what the king did not know was that Captain Kilo was a thief. Not long after Kilo's departure, the king discovered that Captain Kilo had been stealing gold from his treasury. This infuriated him! He ordered that his ships be ready to set sail. "Bring him back," he commanded his men, "with his head chopped off!" But it was too late. Kilo had long disappeared without a trace, and with the king's gold.

On the other hand, Captain Thaddeus Greybellow continued to fight battles at sea and was honored with medals of bravery and titles of grandeur. He became a hero to his nations' people.

At a ball given in his honor by all the heads of state from European and other nations, Greybellow met and fell in love with Lady Kynan. The time came to marry, and Lady Kynan departed from her homeland the Madeira Islands and sailed north across the Atlantic Ocean to become Greybellow's wife. It was during this voyage that Captain Kilo attacked her ship, *The Black Widow*. To escape torture and cruelty, she hid below deck in a straw crate. When the battle was over, Captain Kilo finished his attack by crashing the ship into the reefs up to her bow. At the time, he did not know that the ship carried Lady Kynan as wells as the magic ostrich eggs.

Word of the attack soon reached England and Captain Greybellow. The horror and pain he felt when he realized that Lady Kynan could be captured or even killed hardened his heart. Determined to find the pirates who had done this, Greybellow pleaded with the king for a commission to seek out the pirates and destroy them. The king refused, for the return of the magic eggs and his gold took precedence over pursuing whoever killed or captured Lady Kynan. Angry, and without regard to his command, his country, or his king, Greybellow ordered his men to ready his ship, *The Bluebird*, and prepare to sail. Now in exile, Greybellow swore his allegiance to the sea and to seek out the pirates who had attacked Lady Kynan's ship. He would destroy them. Little did he know that the ship he searched for would be *The Black Widow*.

In his search for the pirates, Greybellow started his own war. Stealing was not his way, but the hate in his heart for the king grew. He stole from the merchant ships heading for England that fed the king's treasure. He would teach kings everywhere a lesson. He became a pirate while desperately trying to forget his pain. The riches were plentiful, and loyalty was in abundance among his crew members. But he could not forget the honor and pride he'd once had as a captain in the English Navy. He needed a new meaning for his life. And, for himself, he could not keep the treasures; instead, he gave them to his countrymen who were poor. He pledged his loyalty to the poor and to the poor countries alike. His trust in keeping these people safe became his strength, and that strength stared back at him when he looked in the mirror.

Greybellow's gesture of giving treasure to the poor did not set well with his crew members. Many had given their lives, but survivors who protested often found themselves walking the plank of death. In turn, his countrymen swore their allegiance to Greybellow out of gratitude, and many became pirates under his command. After many years at sea, the time of stealing and foraging was near the end. Greybellow's hunt for Captain Kilo and the killers had been in vain.

It was late in the day when a sailor from high in the crow's nest spotted a dark fog rolling in toward the ship. It was moving directly into their path, engulfing them in a thick, dark green mist of water. The crew was terrified to hear the sounds of a woman crying, as if in mourning, coming from within the mist. The mist held the ship tight as it sailed directly into the center.

"No turning back now!" a sailor yelled. "Turn her broadside and put her sheets to the wind!"

Another yell came from the crow's nest high on the mast, "Captain, sir, a ship starboard!"

Captain Greybellow, at the helm, raised his spyglass and saw a ship on the horizon of the mist.

"Bring her around for a closer look!" the captain yelled.

Closer she came. Greybellow gave orders to prepare for a fight and board the ship. *Could this be the mighty ship,* The Black Widow? *I have been searching for her so long! Is Captain Kilo on her, or is he still the coward he always was . . . still out on the open seas somewhere?* the captain thought.

Slowly *The Bluebird* turned and came alongside the mystery ship. The men swung from the masts, waving their swords and shouting, "Away with ya! Death to all!" Dropping ladders over the railings of the two ships, they crawled over the water to board the enemy. As waves of cannon balls flew from ship to ship, other sailors swung across on ropes waving their swords and fighting with pistols in hand. The battle continued until surrender or death was imminent. Captain Greybellow jumped aboard, sword in one hand and pistol in the other, fighting off all who were in his path. When it was clear that *The Bluebird* crew had won the battle, the men rounded up the prisoners and secured them on deck. Then Captain Greybellow gave orders to search the ship.

From belowdecks a sailor yelled, "Captain, sir, you need to come below. There's something you need to see."

"Aye, sailor, just what is it I need to see?" said the captain as he leaned over the edge of the hatch.

"Ya better see for yourself, sir," stated the sailor.

Greybellow climbed down the steps of the ladder. On the lower level, he saw barrels of ale, baskets with their contents tumbled out, and treasure chests with their lids open. Alongside the barrels of ale were layers of seaweed, crawling with ocean creatures.

"What is it I need to see, sailor? Isn't this the booty we were looking for?" questioned Greybellow.

"Aye, sir, but over here," the sailor said, pointing with his sword.

Within the ruins of a straw crate lay the body of a woman. She was dressed in green velvet, and her long golden-red hair draped across the edge of the crate. Still hanging around her neck was a locket. Greybellow bent down, picked it up, and held it in his palm. Frightened, he gave the order for everyone to get back. Standing in the light of the open hatch, he slowly opened the locket. There was the face of his mother on one side and his own on the other. It was the locket his mother had given to Kynan as a present. Feelings of lost love heightened his pain and misery now that he knew Kynan was gone for sure.

Pulling his sword from his belt, with terror in his heart and eyes, he waved his trusty weapon, cutting, and lunging at the crew that stood before him.

"Crazy he is!" one was heard to say as they rushed up the ladder to get out of his way. Only those who were on deck or high in the rigging escaped the terror. Falling again to his knees, Greybellow swore once more on the soul of his beloved to make the villains pay. *The Black Widow* would be his ship now. Any secrets it carried would be his. The ostrich eggs and the magic feathers that Captain Kilo had been in search of would be his. The questions really were, did Kilo know they were on board, and where was he now?

On a dark, cloudy day when the seas were high and the wind blew hard, a horrific waterspout came roaring up from the depths of the seas. It picked *The Black Widow* up from the waters like a bird's feather blowing in the wind and carried it across the seas onto land high above the treetops and past the Caves of Wind. It sliced its way through the hollow rocks and landed the ship in the mud pit of our southern regional lands where it remained for centuries.

The cargo was turned upside down. Boxes opened, barrels of ale spilled, and treasures of gold and wares scattered over the hull of the ship. Crates filled with golden eggs, wrapped in parchment and tied with rib-bone strings were tossed and rolled beneath the rubble. For here the precious cargo would lie for years to come.

It was during this time that Captain Greybellow himself was thrown about the ship's deck becoming entangled in ropes and chains that were attached to the mast. The rolling of the ship tossed him high into the air as the chains and ropes continued to wrap around the mast, securing him to it from head to toe and holding him prisoner for eternity. As the chains tightened, they sliced into his skin. His screams of pain rang out over the waves as his last thoughts turned to his beloved. In the end, he was left for the birds, which picked his flesh apart. Some sailors were thrown to the east and some to the west—all except one: Zang remained onboard. He would become the Guardian.

In their search for *The Black Widow* and its treasures, many adventurers disappeared without a trace. Those who were found went mad and told stories of pirate ghosts that chased them with swords and muskets ready to cut their heads off with one big swing. "Mad they were!" said the old timer.

You see, at the time of day when it's really not day or night, people have heard eerie sounds coming from the mud pit. Some say it is the captain crying out. But, if you look really hard, you can see a pair of empty, black, piercing eyes with black blood oozing out looking back at you and just waiting for you to make a move . . . daring you to come his way! Are you ready?

CHAPTER 1

J ERRY FLANAGAN SPENT much of his time reading books about pirates, and especially about the adventures of Captain Greybellow. He knew there was truth to the legends; after all, he had heard the cries of Greybellow himself!

Once, when riding deep in the marshlands and when the morning mist turned to fog, he actually thought he saw Captain Greybellow tied to a mast with chains rattling and ropes flying in the air. At night when lightning strikes across the sky you could see the captain's black, empty eyes staring out. You could hear his screams, because they were louder than the howling wind. The sound would pierce your ears. He had heard all the scary stories, and now Captain Greybellow and his ship *The Black Widow* haunted him in his dreams every night . . .

Nevertheless, Jerry loved taking his bike to the salt marshes where the adventures were just waiting to happen. *Once he fought a tiger from India that escaped from a zoo,* remembered Jerry as he pedaled along. *A fight to the finish it was. I cracked my whip as his claws ripped my skin and moved him back into his cage.*

"What an adventure I had, the tiger and me? Yep, animals and the forest, that's what I really love."

Today is a good day to skip school and go on a new adventure, Jerry thought. *The tree house in the forest, that's where I'll go. No one will find me there. I've got food and I'm off! Besides, tomorrow I meet up with the gang, and they expect me to have a new adventure to tell at the campsite while we roast the dogs. I have a reputation to maintain, so I'd better make it a good one.* Jerry rode his bike down the street and headed for the woods. There were many trails made by animals and hikers along the river near the forest, but there was one trail that no one knew. Only Jerry knew the trail, for he had made it himself. It was midmorning when he reached the end of K–2 trail. As he looked for his markers, he realized that all the trees seemed to have grown. *There's the marker on the old elm,* he thought. Right where its limbs reached the ground, the emblem of two crosses was etched in the trunk. *The marks are deep, just as I carved them when I was nine,* Jerry thought to himself. That had been three years ago, and no one had found them. *The cover is excellent. Better hide the bike. The walk will be long, and there's no need for someone to take it.* He pushed back the underbrush and laid his bike deep under the forest floor covering it to give the appearance that animals had been sleeping there.

Learned that trick from Uncle Bud, I'd better make a marker and place it on top of the brush so I can find it, he thought.

He tore the corner off a holly leaf and creased it into the shape of a heart. *That's perfect! Couldn't be better if Bud*

2

did it himself, let's see . . . where is my backpack? There it is. He picked it up, and off he went down the trail to look for the next two crosses.

It had been a while since he had been on the trail, and everything had grown. There were more vines and leaves. The trees seemed taller. There had been lots of rain that spring, and the growth in the forest really looked good and healthy. He walked slowly, climbing between rocks and along the narrow path. He stopped when he found two more crosses carved on a tree trunk. *Let's see . . . where are the rocks?* He dug and pushed until he found three rocks that formed an arrow. Now he knew what direction to go. He continued down the narrow path pulling limbs and vines back out of his way. Deeper and deeper into the forest he went, not ever suspecting that all the signs he had placed had been moved. The trail now was leading him straight for the Caves of Wind and for the hollow rocks.

Jerry stumbled as he clambered over the hollow rocks. The rocks made echoing sounds with his every step. Suddenly, he realized he was lost. Scratching his head and pulling his jeans up, he stopped to think. *The signs I put in place were still there, but something fishy is going on.* Shrugging his shoulders and scratching his head, he continued walking through the hollow rocks when he heard something. "Who's there?" he called out. "Hello, anyone there?" He stopped to listen.

It sounded like a cry coming from inside the rocks. "There it is again," he said out loud—loud enough for anyone to hear him. He decided to move at a faster pace and continued to follow the rock formations and the arrows he had put in place. *Strange . . . I don't remember all the rocks and mud,* he thought. *There hasn't been that much rain lately. There it is again . . . the "cry" . . . where is it coming from?* As fear built, his mind continued to stray.

Trying to follow the sound of crying, he went deeper and deeper into the forest. With each step he took, the cry seemed to close in on him. It became stronger as he stumbled and fell into mud—mud that was deep. The mud became tight and closed in around his body and legs. Pulling his arms out of the mud, he reached to grab a limb hanging from a tree.

"I can do this! Pull hard and hold on tight!" he screamed as he tried to pull himself to safety. The cries got louder. Holding on as tight as he could, he turned and looked toward the horizon of the mud pit. And there it was—a ship! The cries seemed to be coming from the ship. He could hear clanging sounds of metal as the wind blew. He could see chains and ropes flying high entangled in cobwebs that stretched from bow to stern. Pulling down on the limb with all his might, he started to pull himself out of the mud. A slip sent him back into the pit, but he held on tight. The mud was slippery, and he was covered with icky green slime. Pulling hand over hand, he pulled himself out of the mud, struggled to his feet, and stretched tall to see the ship again.

"Is it still there?" he said out loud. Dripping in mud and green slime, he gathered his things and continued his journey and headed for the ship. "Wow, what a find!"

When he reached the side of the ship, he carefully climbed aboard. He was amazed. "Struck it rich, I have!" he said aloud. *A real pirate ship*, he thought, looking around. *I wonder where it came from. How did it get here? Wow, what a neat ship!*

He could see that the bow was stuck in the mud and that the stern rose up and down in the mud. He looked over the side of the ship and there he saw shiny gold letters with slime and mud all over them. He took his jackknife from his pocket, stood on his toes and leaned over the side where the rail was broken, and scraped the mud off one of the letters. It was a *B*. Then one by one he scraped more letters: *L, A, C, K*. "What kind of ship is this?" he asked out loud as he continued to scrape the mud. "*The Black Widow!*" he cried.

This must be the ship that the old timer in town tells stories about, he thought. *It's real! We can make the new hideout here! Won't the gang be surprised when they see the ship! I'll make some signs so I can find my way back. Crossbones with a skull, that's it. I'll make a skull and crossbones every fifty feet or so down the trail. The first one will be on the mast so I'll be able to see it from a distance.*

While Jerry marked the mast, a set of piercing eyes was watching him from high above the sails. There he sat in the crow's nest, waiting and guiding, making sure each skull and crossbones was in its proper place. "I won't let him make any mistakes, for it has taken too long and they will be here soon and will set me free."

Jerry reached the edge of the path and slept until the next morning. He uncovered his bike and rode down the trail toward the old oak tree where the gang was to meet. "I can't wait to tell 'em about the pirate ship—*The Black Widow*," he screamed out as he rode down the trail.

His adventure had been much more than he had expected, and a new adventure with the gang was going to be glorious. It was summer, and the gang had a new hideout and a new campsite. What could be better than that! *The Black Widow* would be their ship. They would sail her, and pirates they would be. Could just hear them saying, "Aye aye, sir!" What fun this was going to be.

CHAPTER 2

ITWAS SUMMER, riding down the hill feeling free as the wind. The speed of his new bike was more than he expected. It was a black and blue racer. All the kids would know who had the power to ride the wind. He raced past the light poles, the houses, and the trees. He felt a strong urge to head for the woods and the river. The Falls, that's the place, I'll go. I can smell the water, taste the wind, and feel the speed! The racer can take me anywhere I want to go!

The buzzer on the alarm clock sounded, and Sam woke from his dream *"That darn alarm clock, I hate it! It's Saturday morning! I should get to sleep late and dream of wonderful things to come, like my speed racer!* He lay back on his pillow with his arms folded under his head. *Besides, what a dream!* He turned over to go back to sleep.

"Sam! Breakfast!" yelled Sam's mom from the bottom of the stairs. "Better hurry—today starts the campout, and you don't want to be late."

"Heck, I almost forgot!" He kicked the bed covers off his feet. *I'd better hurry!* Sam jumped out of bed and pulled his favorite jeans from the chest of drawers. *The jeans with holes in the knees and my favorite shirt with the big pockets, yep that is the attire of the day. Where are those tennis shoes? I know they've got to be here somewhere. Where did I put 'em? There you are—ah, come out from under there. One shoe, then the other. Socks, ugh, put 'em on later. Got to hurry . . . running late.*

Down the stairs Sam ran, yelling, "Gotta run, Mom, no time to eat!"

"You come back here and eat your breakfast, Sam."

"No thanks, Mom, can't—no time! See ya later!"

Out the door he ran, tumbling down the steps into the rosebushes.

Oh, that's smart! Better not *let Mom see; she won't let me go. Hum, another hole in my jeans. Cool. Now I have twelve holes, and that's a new record.* Up he got, strapped his backpack on, grabbed his bike, and rode off toward Joey's house.

Joey was Sam's best friend. They had always been there for each other, even when Kevin Sims blackened Sam's eye and Valerie Chart punched Joey in the stomach. *Eight years now, best friends, and still tight,* he thought.

Joey's house was full of laughter. He had three older sisters, and he was the only brother. His sisters were always pulling tricks on him. One time they dressed him up in little girl's clothes and pretended he was their baby. Joey hated it, but he loved his sisters and played along. *Wish I had sisters just like his,* thought Sam.

Sam finally arrived at Joey's house. Joey's room was upstairs, and as usual the window was open. "Hey—Joey, hurry up! It's Saturday, and we're late. All the guys will be waiting," yelled Sam vigorously.

"I'm coming—hold your shirt tails!" Joey yelled from the upstairs window.

Soon, a large, robust, red haired, big-cheeked boy burst through the front door. His feet covered the porch, and his smile covered both sides of his face.

Joey was fun-loving and the greatest pal a guy could have. He always wore the same black shorts and red shirt. His sneakers were black-and-white checked with a blue edge. He wore his shoes on the wrong feet so that everyone could read "Red Baron," his hero!

"Hey, Sam, I'm ready," said Joey with a grin. "Got donuts and a *huge* supply of Wonder Cakes, so I'm set." Sam never did understand what Joey saw in Wonder Cakes. The darn things taste like metal cans and smelled like cat poo! But he always had one in his shirt pocket, and boy did he love to eat them.

"Let's ride by and pick up Tom and Cal, and then we're off. Only have an hour or so to get there, Joey," said Sam. "Don't want to keep Jerry waiting," he finished in a hurried breath.

Tom and Cal were on their way when they met up with Sam and Joey. The four of them stopped and were busy talking about the upcoming day when Sally—known as Big Sal to the gang—showed up. She was a mighty big girl for her age. The boys tried to ride off, but Big Sal grabbed the handlebars of Tom's and Cal's bikes and stopped them dead in their tracks. Sam and Joey tried to ride off as fast as they could and headed for the old oak tree.

Cal felt a huge lump in his throat as he stared straight into Big Sal's eyes. Just thinking about what she would do scared him to death. Sally was not someone you'd say no to without consequences. There was no telling what she would do from one moment to the next. Once she had tied Hank Thompson to a light post with his own jeans just because he refused to let her pass on his side of the sidewalk.

"Hope she doesn't kill me when we tell her she can't go with us on the campout," Cal whispered to Tom.

"Good morning, Cal! Where are you going this bright, lovely morning? Don't you just love my new dress? Don't ya just love it?" Sally gestured for the boys to look at her new dress. Big Sal had a crush on the boys, and they knew that this wasn't the morning to tell her that her new dress made her look like the broad side of a barn with advertisement for pig feed.

"Big Sal—I mean Sally—your new dress is love-r-lee, but we've got to go and meet up with Jerry. He's waiting," Cal said with a wavy voice of terror.

"Where ya going, Cal?" asked Sal.

"Can't tell ya, it's top secret. If I tell ya, the guys . . . they'll kill me," Cal responded with fear in his voice.

That was not what Sal wanted to hear. She was used to getting her way, and there was only one way to deal with this situation, so she took a big breath.

"Oh, no, not that, Sally!" said Cal. "I know that look!" He turned to his friends. "We're in for it now. Duck everyone!"

Then it happened, *the burp! Big Sal could blast the side of a horse's head off and move a thirty-foot tidal wave back to sea with her burps*, thought Tom. *And smell!* He held his nose!

"Uck!" yelled Tom. "Is there food on my face or neck? Look out! Oh no, there she blows! Run for cover everyone!"

Then a sound that only Sally could make came from her mouth: "Bleshshsheshehen!"

"Okay! You can come, Sally. Just stop! The guys are going to kill me," said Cal.

⁂

Sally Warner was a girl not to be messed with. She was the youngest of four rowdy kids and always had to fight for attention. Her three brothers had picked on her from the time she was old enough to walk. One day, when she was five, she was eating cabbage and ham hocks and burped so loudly and strongly that her brothers laughed themselves silly. She learned very quickly that the more she burped the more attention she got. The sounds she could make with her burps were indescribable. She also learned that the burping could be a weapon of sorts. One day at the dinner table, she got tired of being picked on and decided to strike back the only way she knew how. She inhaled so much air into her lungs that her cheeks blew up like large red balls. Then out it came! Food went flying and landed on her brothers. She inhaled again and sent out another blast of air like a hurricane, pushing their eyelids back to their foreheads. Each time, her attack would get stronger, and off they would go, running for their lives. With a smile on her face, for the first time she knew she had a way to fight back, and from then on, she used it as a weapon to get her way.

When it came time to go to school, she had already developed into a bully using her burp weapon. Then she met Jerry, Tom, Cal, Sam, and Joey. These guys were her heroes. They had so much fun. They were real buddies—always sticking up for one another, and that was what she wanted: real friends. All she wanted to do was to hang out with them. She just didn't know how to make them believe she was their buddy too. They always got on the wrong side of her and forced her to burp.

The meeting place was the old oak tree on Fifth and Elm. It was almost ten o'clock, and Joey had begun to wonder where everyone was. "Where's Jerry?" he asked Sam. "He promised to be here. It's important! Jerry is the only one who knows how to get to the secret hideout at Black Scar Patch."

"Here come Cal and Tom," said Joey. "What is Sally doing with them?"

"Joey, we're in trouble now." Sam shook his head.

Tom was Cal's younger brother by eighteen months, but they looked like twins. Even their mom sometimes had a hard time telling them apart. The only way their friends could tell them apart was that Tom's right ear was bigger than the left and at the top corner was a scar that looked like a star. Tom was great at digging up neat things to do, but Cal, on the other hand, could not fight his way out of a brown paper bag that had been buried under ten pounds of bird doo. They were so different yet so much the same. They lifted weights and ran every day. The guys could always depend on Tom's strength to get them through tough times and out of hard places. Cal tried so hard to be like Tom.

"Look—it's Jerry!" yelled Tom. "He made it!" All the guys admired Jerry and thought he was the bravest kid in town. One time, he hid in the principal's office under the principal's desk and farted. The principal never knew he was there. He called his secretary into the office and ordered her to have the place sprayed. The kids in school laughed and laughed. He really could come up with cool things and get away with them.

Jerry's mom and his uncle were raising him. Jerry wasn't sure what had happened to his dad. His uncle was a woodsman and taught him lots of cool stuff about the trees and rocks in the forest. He taught Jerry about animals and their habits and how to fix stuff with only a few tools and materials. Some folks said that Jerry grew up in the forest and was raised by animals. He was so smart about the ways of the forest. *What a guy*, thought Sam!

"Hey, Jerry, we're here, and ready!" Joey spoke with excitement.

"What's Sally doing here?" asked Jerry. "The campout is for guys only." He turned to Sally. "Sal, you aren't coming with us. You just can't come, Sal!"

"And who is going to stop me, Mr. Smarty Pants?" said Sal. "I can do anything I want to, and you can't stop me. Just like the time I jumped off the radio tower—one hundred feet, remember Jerry? No one could stop me then either."

"Yeah, I remember," grumbled Jerry, "and I remember picking cattle berries in Yuma too. No girls! Did you hear me? No girls!"

Sal's face turned red, her chest blew up three sizes, and her fist was so tight you could see the blood in her veins ready to pop.

"Everyone *run!* She's going to explode!" yelled Sam.

"Take cover!" yelled Tom. Bikes came crashing to the ground. Tennis shoes went in every direction. Legs went flying behind bushes.

But not Jerry; he stood his ground. He stood opposite Sal. Face to face and nose to nose they stood, their eyes piercing into each other's brains.

"Her brains are going to spew all over the place," said Joey.

From behind the bushes and trees they watched as Sally's face reddened and her cheeks grew bigger.

"They are going to explode!" yelled Cal.

"Don't be silly, Cal. Her ears will blow off first," said Tom.

"No, they won't! Her brains will become marbles and they will shoot up like hot air balloons," replied Joey.

That's when Jerry did the ultimate. "Put a cork in it, Sal! You're not going, and that's final. Your burping doesn't do it for me."

Sal opened her mouth, and out came a sound that was louder than the ships' foghorns they heard out on the ocean. Jerry held his hands up in front of his face as his hair blew backward until you could see his scalp ripple. His eyes were pushed back, and his nose turned up like a pig's. What a sight!

Jerry stood fast. When Sally finished her burp, he reached into his pocket and pulled out a plastic egg. He opened it and took out a wad of Silly Putty. Looking at Sal, he stuck the Silly Putty into her mouth. He slammed shut her jaw. Sal's eyes bulged so wide she looked like a bullfrog.

"Now," said Jerry, "as I said, you are not going, and that's that! If you don't stop being a pain, I am going to take these baby frogs I've got here in my pocket and put them down your dress!"

Sally coughed, gasped, and spit out the Silly Putty. "Oh, yeah?" she said, and she swelled up again. Jerry took a piece of rope out of his back pocket. Before Sal realized what he was doing, he backed her up to the old oak tree and tied her up! Then he really did it—he dropped all the baby frogs down inside her new dress.

Out came the boys running, jumping, and yelling. "He won!" sang Cal, echoed by his brother. "He Won! Boy, Jerry, you are so brave," said Sam.

Off they went laughing and chanting, "Jerry is the champion!"

"To the forest!" Jerry yelled back, and they rode off on their bikes, leaving Sally screaming and kicking—and stuck!

CHAPTER 3

WHEN THE GANG reached the edge of the forest, Jerry slowed down to a stop, held up his hand, and yelled, "Stop, guys. I have lots to tell you! You aren't going to believe what I found—a new hideout!"

"Aren't we going to our hideout at Black Scare Patch?" asked Sam, sounding confused.

"Man, I'm ready to ride the trails!" screamed Cal.

"Me too!" hollered Tom.

"My Wonder Cakes won't melt, will they?" Joey asked, sounding bewildered.

Jerry whistled through his front teeth as loudly as he could, and all eyes and ears were on him. "Listen up! I found *The Black Widow.*"

"*The Black Widow?* What's that?" asked Tom. "I've never heard of *The Black Widow.* Are you talking about a giant spider?"

"No, stupid! It's a *pirate ship!*"

"Remember the old timer who tells stories on the corner of Tenth and State? Remember his pirate stories? Well they're real! I found the ship!"

"You've got to be kidding," said Cal. "Where, out in the marshlands?"

"Come on—I'll show you. You won't believe your eyes," Jerry said with excitement. "It's our new hideout!"

Down K-2 trail they rode, faster and faster, not knowing what was lying ahead of them: Jerry, Sam, Joey, Cal and Tom—a team ready for adventure.

At the end of the trail, they skidded to a stop. Tom asked, "What do we do now? We can't take our bikes any farther. The forest is too thick, and how much farther do we have to go anyway, Jerry?"

"We'll hide the bikes over there." Jerry pointed to a small slender path where the crossbone markings on the tree were etched. "Everyone, gather vines, leaves, brush, and anything else you can find to help cover the bikes. Then gather your camping gear and backpacks, and we'll walk the rest of the way. Besides it isn't much farther. It's near the mud pit, but we need to hurry." Jerry found the rocks that were arranged in the form of an arrow and pointed in the direction of the caves. He turned and started to walk. "This way to the pirate ship!" he called over his shoulder.

The day was warming up, and the boys were becoming overheated from walking so long on the trail. Joey's thirst began to crawl in his throat as well as hunger in his stomach.

"Can we stop soon and eat? I'm starved," he complained.

"We'll stop when we find the crosses and arrows on the next tree. They point the way," answered Jerry.

In an hour or so, they located the crosses and arrows, and Joey's first Wonder Cake came squishing out of his pocket.

"Joey, pass one of those metal cakes over here," said Sam.

"I could do with a bite," suggested Tom as he licked his lips.

"Thought you didn't like Wonder Cakes," Joey said as he took the first bite and then shared the rest with his buddies. Everyone agreed the Wonder Cakes tasted like metal, but it satisfied their stomachs. Tom and Joey were horsing around while Sam was showing Cal the cool watch he had bought at the swap meet. Pushing and shoving, they fell to the ground wrestling and laughing. Horsing around was one of their favorite pastimes. Cal rolled over laughing and started to sit up when he caught something in the corner of his eye.

"Look at the arrow on that tree trunk. Hey, guys, stop!"

Stuck to the crosses on the trunk of the tree was a rolled-up piece of golden paper with a rib-bone strings tied around it. Recognizing the strings that the local fisherman made from the shells of oysters, Tom reached up and tore the little scroll off the crosses and handed it to Cal. Turning the golden paper over where the rib-bone strings were tied in a rather unusual bow, he began to untie the strings one by one. When he opened the golden paper, the smell of decay filled the air. Jerry pulled the paper out of Cal's hands.

"Give it back!" yelled Cal.

"I can read it just fine," smarted off Jerry.

"Stop arguing, Cal. Go ahead and read what it says, Jerry," said Tom. "It's no big deal, Cal."

Jerry's voice shook a little as he read:

> The awareness of seven will lead you to power.
> Truth lies in the jaws of a yak.

"What does that mean?" asked Sam.

"I don't know," Jerry replied.

"Maybe it's a riddle," Cal said. "I'm good at riddles." Cal pulled the golden paper out of Jerry's hands and read it again. The paper blazed red and became hot! Cal dropped it suddenly. "It burned my hand!" he said.

"Yeah, yeah," cautioned Jerry. "Yeah, it just stung a bit." Jerry picked the paper up from the ground only to find it was cool to touch. He stuck it into his pocket, and no more was said. They set off again for their hideout.

The trail was narrow, and the air was hot. The trail was thick with ferns, bushes, and brush. Everyone was hot and ready for a break. Jerry pointed to the Caves of the Wind. "Up there," he said. "We'll stop there." Barely were the words out of his mouth when Joey stumbled and tumbled into a deep, wide hole.

"My leg! It's stuck!" screamed Joey. His leg was caught between two big tree roots, which were covered with thick layers of mud. Try as he might, he was unable to pull himself free. He screamed and screamed with fear. The gang reached down the hole and tried pulling him up, but his leg was stuck fast and would not come free. Joey was scared and would not stop screaming.

"Okay, okay—stop! Stop screaming, Joey," yelled Cal. "We'll think of something!"

Settling back from the edge of the hole and laying their backpacks down, they decided it would be best to assess the problem and see what could be done.

"Joey, stop screaming! You hear me?" said Cal. "Sam, do you have one of Joey's Wonder Cakes?"

"Yeah."

"Then toss it down to him." He leaned over the edge of the hole. "Eat this, Joey. It'll calm you down." The boys sat back down to think while Joey ate his cake.

"Sam, if we link our belts together," suggested Jerry, "we can make a rope. We can throw the end of the belt over that tree branch, and use it as a leverage to pull him out. Tom and Cal, you climb down into the hole, dig the mud out from around his leg, then we'll pull him up."

"Good idea, just get me out!" yelled Joey. The boys quickly removed their belts and connected them together. Jerry tied a rock to the end as a weight and then threw it over a large, sturdy tree limb. Tugging to see if it was secure, he dropped it down the hole. Tom and Cal jumped into the hole even though it was a tight fit.

"Joey, put the belt under your shoulders and hook a loop around you," instructed Sam. "It's secure. Try to pull yourself up."

"Stop!" yelled Jerry as Joey began to pull at the makeshift rope. "He's going to break the tree limb!"

"Can you break the roots apart, Tom?" Jerry yelled. Tom pushed on one root with his foot while Cal pulled on the other. One of the roots finally broke. "Now dig around Joey's leg with any sticks you can find," suggested Jerry.

"We've dug most of the mud out," Tom called out. "Try to pull him up!"

"Okay, Sam, pull with all your might!" screeched Jerry.

After a few minutes, Joey's leg came free from the mud with a great sucking noise. He was covered in mud and gunk.

With everyone's help, Joey finally found himself sitting on the ground above the hole wiping mud from his arms and legs. Everyone was laughing at the different sounds his feet made. But all Joey could do was think, *No matter what, friends like these guys . . . well there just aren't any other guys like 'em in the world.*

"Hey, Joey, look something is stuck to the bottom of your shoe!" said Sam.

"Where did that come from?" said Joey as he bent over and pulled a golden scroll of paper tied with rib-bone strings off the bottom of his shoe. I must have picked it up when I climbed out of the hole," said Joey. It looked just like the one Cal found. He turned it over to the side where the strings were and untied them. As he opened it, the smell of decay again filled the air. Joey began to read:

> The awareness of six who are together will show strength in power. Truth lies in the jaws of the yak.

Sam grabbed the golden paper to read it for himself, and found it hot to the touch. He dropped the paper to the ground and Joey smarted off. "See, if you wouldn't be so grabby, it wouldn't have burned you!"

Joey picked up the paper. He found it soothing to the touch and not hot at all. They all remembered that the same thing had happened to Cal.

"Don't you think this is weird, Jerry?" asked Joey. "How did these things get here?"

"I don't know, Joey. Do you really think I have all the answers all the time?" Jerry answered rather abruptly.

"What doesn't make sense is why the pieces of paper burned our hands and not Joey's or Jerry's," said Tom as he shook his head. "Beats me, Joey. But I do think it's time we move on." Tom turned and seemed to see something in the bushes. "Look over there in the bushes!" he whispered in a panic. But by the time they turned, whatever it was had gone.

"What was it, Tom?" Sam said.

"Did you see the eyes?" said Tom shakily. "They were dark and piercing, and made chills go up my spine."

"Oh, Tom, it probably was an animal," explained Sam. "Yeah, a deer. That's what it was. Come on, let's get out of here."

CHAPTER 4

I T WAS AFTERNOON, and everyone was getting tired and hungry again. "Jerry, let's eat. I'm starved," said Sam.

"Me too," announced Joey as he pulled out his Wonder Cakes.

"Oh, Joey, you're always hungry," said Tom.

"By the way, just how many of those cakes do you have?" asked Cal.

"I'll never tell."

Cal shook his head. All agreed to stop at the pool of water below the caves to swim and eat a late lunch. What a treat! The water was cool and jumping off the cliffs would be a blast.

"Cal, bet you can't do a gainer off the cliff," said Tom.

"Man, that's easy," boasted Cal. Off he went, climbing to the top of the cliff. When he got to the top, it looked as if he was a mile high! He looked over the cliff to see the best place to jump, and saw something at the bottom staring up. He froze in place.

"Scaredy-cat, scaredy-cat," yelled several of the boys, laughing.

"Looking for a reason not to jump?" called out Tom.

"Hey, what's that in the water?" Cal asked, pointing downward.

"Nothing!" yelled Sam, looking down. "I don't see anything. It's probably the reflection of the holes in the clouds."

"Yeah, you're probably right," answered Cal. He looked up into the sky.

Now it wasn't jumping off the cliff that scared Cal, it was going under the water so deep. He had always had the fear that he might not come up. His brother Tom gave him confidence by simply being there. Tom was a better swimmer than the rest of the boys. Last summer he had competed in the national swim/dive meet and won all the first-place ribbons. He'd never been beaten! He could hold his breath forever! *I will be safe.*

Cal stepped to the edge of the cliff, took a deep breath, swung his arms out, and jumped as high and far out as he could go. Closing his eyes tight and grabbing his legs with his arms, he could feel the weight of gravity pulling him down toward the water. All he could think about was Tom and how he would save him. He hit the water with a huge splash, and down he went, deeper and deeper. He could feel his shorts fill up with water as the air bubbles floated through his underpants and up and over his chest and face. The tickling sensation was a very weird feeling. When his feet hit the bottom, Cal opened his eyes and turned to push off the bottom toward the surface. But he was surprised to see what he saw. There it stood—taller than he and as wide as he could see. It was huge, and it was moving toward him. What was it? The eyes were black and piercing like round, hard rocks. *I've got to get out of here!* thought Cal. Bending knees and preparing to push off and swim upwards, he realized he couldn't move. His pants were caught on something, and he couldn't shake them loose. He pulled and tugged, but was unable to free himself. *I'm going to die. I just know I'm doomed. Where is Tom?* The thing with the scary eyes came closer and closer. Cal's fears heighten. *The air in my lungs is going to explode? I can't pull free!* All of a sudden, a hand reached down and grabbed him, and up to the top of the water they came.

"Help me!" said Tom as he dragged his brother to the rocks at the edge of the pool. "He's unconscious!"

Everyone jumped in the water and helped to pull Cal to safety. Jerry pulled him up the bank, and Tom turned him over on his stomach and pushed up and down on his back. It took three times before the water came spewing out his mouth. Cal choked and grasped for air, but he was okay.

"Turn him over on his back," said Tom.

"Wow, man, we thought you were a goner," said Sam.

"Cal, sure you're okay, brother?" said Tom.

"You scared us to death," said Joey. "What happened down there?"

"I landed on my butt, and I guess got the air knocked out of me," explained Cal. "And somehow I got caught."

"Tom jumped in and brought you up out of the water. He saved you!" explained Jerry.

"Did you see it down there, Tom?" asked Cal.

"See what?" asked Tom.

"It stood seven foot tall and had dark eyes."

"No, man, I just jumped in, dove down, grabbed your arm and pulled you up. I didn't see anything."

"But my pants! They were stuck!"

"No they weren't."

Cal looked at his butt pocket so he could show Tom the rip. He was sure it would be there. But all he saw was that his pocket hanging on by threads, and stuck inside the ripped pocket was a piece of golden paper with rib-bone strings. It was just like the ones Joey and Jerry had got.

"Where did that come from?" questioned Tom.

"Heck if I know," said Cal as his voice shivered. Cal pulled it out of his pocket, untied the rib-bone strings and read:

> The awareness of five in brotherhood will find power to show the way. Truth lies in the jaws of the yak.

As he read the message, he began to understand the true meaning of brotherhood. A sense of peace came over him, and for the first time he was glad he had a brother and understood the importance of friends.

"What's it say?" asked Sam. He became angry and grabbed the note away from Cal. "There is something weird going on here, and I'm going to get down to just what it is!" declared Sam. As he began to read it for himself, the paper began to burn his palms and fingers. Throwing it down he screamed, "It's haunted! Something is out there watching us. Can't you feel it?" Sam's anger had turned to fear.

Turning and looking at one another, one at a time, they began to scream. No one knew why they were screaming, but they were. Scrambling to pick up their clothes, they went running, putting one leg after the other into their pants, and trying to pull them up at the same time. They needed to get out of there. As Cal grabbed his shirt and picked up the note, he wondered what all these messages meant. Looking up all he could see were swinging arms and stumbling legs being shoved into pant legs. "Hey! Wait for me!" Tucking the piece of paper into his front pocket, he took off to catch up with the others.

They ran as fast as their legs could carry them, grabbing backpacks and anything else their hands touched. They ran straight up for the Caves of Wind. Once inside, everyone collapsed to the ground. Out of breath and feeling weird, they just stared. Their thoughts were on the golden papers and the messages.

"They must mean something," said Sam finally. "What are we going to do, Jerry?"

"Why should I always be the one to decide?"

"You brought us here, didn't you? And all this happened because you wanted—"

Tom interrupted, "Oh, come on, Jerry. This is pretty weird stuff, don't you think?"

"Let's read the messages again. Maybe there's a clue," Cal jumped in. The gang removed their backpacks and gathered together as the boys pulled the notes out of their pockets and sat down to read them. "Jerry, you first," said Cal.

Solemnly, Jerry read:

> The awareness of seven will lead you to power.
> The truth lies in the jaws of the yak.

"Okay," said Cal. "Joey your turn."

Joey's voice shook as he read:

The awareness of six who are together will show strength in power. Truth lies in the jaws of the yak.

Cal took his turn to read:

> The awareness of five in brotherhood will find power to show the way. Truth lies in the jaws of the yak.

"I wonder what 'truth lies in the jaws of the yak' means?" wondered Joey. "And what is a yak anyway?"

"It's in each one," said Tom. "I think a yak is like a big cow or buffalo."

"Really, a cow, Tom?" said Joey in disbelief. "But the number just gets smaller as if someone is counting off backward."

"Good clue, Joey," said Sam.

"You know, when I was on the pirate ship," said Jerry, "it felt like someone was always watching me. Cal, you thought someone or something was in the water when you jumped, right?"

Cal nodded. "Yeah, there's something going on. Maybe when we get to the pirate ship we can figure this out. Let's think on it," said Jerry.

They all settled back against rocks and broken-up tree trunks. The boys who had received the messages held the golden pieces of paper up to the light coming from the opening of the cave and investigated their message for clues, hidden words, or secret symbols—anything that would help them understand.

"We'd better get started again," said Jerry. "We need to get through the hollow rocks beyond the caves before dark.

CHAPTER 5

T HEY WERE APPROACHING the hollow rocks, and found it an easy climb. The rocks gave off an echo sound when people walked over them. That is how the area got its name.

Joey felt the effort of the climb, and his stomach growled. He thought, *One more Wonder Cake, and I could make it.* Jerry led the way followed by Cal, Tom, Joey, and then Sam. Joey stepped up on a rock then moved to another and farted a big long one that echoed through the hollow rocks. Everyone laughed until they forgot about the notes. They forged through the rocks climbing higher. At the top of the hill they saw the mud pit.

"It won't be long now," said Jerry. "We'd've been there by now if we hadn't stopped to goof off."

Down the trail at the backside of the hill they marched. Jerry could feel the wind build and see the trees bending in the distance.

"A storm is brewing," he advised. "We'd better walk faster or we're going to get caught in the wind." But before they could get much farther, the wind came up and started blowing bits of sand in their eyes and mouths. It burned their eyes, and tasted vile. The wind grew stronger.

"Keep close and stay down!" ordered Jerry. Grains of sand blew up from the ground with greater speed forming small whirlwinds. Everyone was coughing and rubbing their eyes.

"We've got to get out of the wind!" yelled Tom. "The sand and pebbles will rip our skin to shreds."

"Over there!" said Sam, pointing. "See it? A cave! Let's go!" One by one they entered the small cave wiping dirt and sand from their eyes and trying to spit the sand out of their mouths. They settled down to wait the storm out. It was late in the day, and they decided to stay for the night. It would be safer. The hollow rocks formed many caves, and they were neat to hang out in. The wind whistled through them and made neat sounds too.

"How long do you think it will be before we get out of here, Jerry?" asked Joey. "I'm hungry!"

"Better go easy on the Wonder Cakes," stated Sam. "There's no way to tell when we'll get back."

"We always kept food stashed at the tree house," said Joey. "If we were there we could have a feast! That's where we were supposed to go to begin with. It's a cool place! Jerry, even your Uncle Bud thought we did a super job building it. Wish we went to the tree house instead."

"Oh, don't be such a scaredy-cat, Joey. Nothing is going to happen, not as long as I am here," said Sam patting Joey on the shoulder.

Tom started to wander to the back of the cave. "Neat! There's another section back here," he called to the others. "Cal, let's check it out! Anyone know how to make a torch?"

"Yeah, I do," said Cal. "Learned in Boy Scouts." Cal rolled some green brush together around the end of a sturdy stick, than applied dry brush over it tightly. He tore off the tail of his shirt and used it to tie the bundle together. Then he took a match from his backpack and lit it. It first smoldered, then flamed. Everyone was very impressed with Cal's skill in making the torch, but he could have done something about the smell.

The others stayed in the front part of the cave while Tom and Cal explored the other section. Although the homemade torch worked, it was still rather dark in the cave. "This is kind of spooky," said Tom as they made their way deeper and deeper in the cave. "I thought it was going to be a cool adventure. Can't really tell what has lived here, but look at those burrows and all that animal hair. An animal den. How neat. Be careful where you step," he continued. "You can't tell what you could step on or into."

Then Cal stepped into poop and yelled, "Tell me about it."

"Cal, remember how we used to draw stick animals on the basement walls pretending we were in a cave?"

"Yeah," said Cal. "And then Dad would jump out in the bearskin? Scared us to death!

"This cave reminds me of those times."

"Yeah, me too, but just a little bit," Cal replied.

"Look, Cal, up on the wall," said Tom. "Hold the torch high—there, you see it? See that arrow? There's a lot of them. Let's follow them and see where they go." The arrows led them to a large grouping of rocks.

Low and behold, another golden piece of paper tied with rib-bone strings was stuck to a rock.

"Jeepers," said Cal. "Open it up, Tom, and read what it says." Cal held the torch and Tom read:

> The awareness of four has found a puzzle to solve.
> The truth lies in the jaws of the yak.

"Wow, Tom, let me see it!" Cal grabbed the note from Tom's hand, and like all the others it too burned his palm and fingertips. He dropped the note and yelled, "It's hot!" The yelling and carrying on brought the others running.

"What is it? What's happened?" yelled Jerry.

"It's another note, and it burned my hands," said Cal.

"What'd it say, Tom?" Tom read the note aloud.

"This is so spooky," said Sam. Four of us have received notes. The only one who hasn't got one is me."

"Guys, we'd better be very careful," said Jerry. "From now on let's stick together. Tom, you and Cal stay together. Sam and Joey and I'll keep the lead. Let's get back and try to get some sleep. In the morning the storm will be over and we'll head for the mud pit.

Moving toward the front of the cave, Joey cried out, "I'm not going! I'm going home! This is all too weird, and I'm scared."

"Joey, you'll be okay," said Sam. "I'll stay close and protect you. You're my buddy, and I won't let anything happen to you, I promise."

"Yea, Joey, I'll be here too," said Cal. "Tom will back us up, and remember how Jerry stood up to Big Sal? We're tough when we stand together. We can do anything if we stick together."

"Come on, Joey," pleaded Cal.

"Okay, okay," said Joey. "But promise me you'll stay close." They all agreed and turned in for the night.

CHAPTER 6

"WAKE UP GUYS! The sun is up!" called Jerry. As they awoke, his buddies rubbed their eyes and yawned.

"What a night" moaned Sam. "Ooh, Joey, your breath smells like dog farts!"

"Quit your complaining," said Joey as he tried to roll over and go back to sleep.

Jerry kicked Tom and Cal, then Joey in the butt with his foot. "Come on, guys, wake up! We need to get a move on. We wasted time yesterday fooling around. We've got to make it before dark. I made it in one day, and it's the second day already. We're wasting time, guys!"

They all gathered their things and started out. Without talking about it, they all knew each of them was thinking about the golden pieces of paper tied with rib-bone strings. Where did they come from? Why were they getting them? Why were they hot one minute, cold another? And what the heck is a yak? The questions in their heads kept twirling around without answers.

"No time to eat," said Jerry. "We'll munch on berries along the trail. Let's get going."

A tree had fallen over the mud pit during the storm. The trunk and limbs were covered with green slime, which also covered the surrounding rocks and ground. It was everywhere, and there was more of it than Jerry had seen before. The fog rose from the mud obscuring their view across the pit, but Jerry knew the ship was there, and he knew he could find it.

"Where is the pirate ship, Jerry?" demanded Sam.

"Over there." Jerry pointed toward the west end of the pit. They stretched their necks, stood on their toes, and looked as hard as they could, but still they could not see the ship.

"I can't see anything," said Joey.

"Me neither," chimed Sam.

"Come on, you'll see it soon enough," mocked Jerry.

The climb over the tree trunk was slippery and much harder than anything they had encountered so far on this adventure. "We have to get through the mud pit before dark," said Jerry, "and it'll take all day to walk through them at the rate we're moving. Maybe it would be better if we hooked our belts together, then around each other so that no one falls or gets lost." Everyone agreed it would be safer. Hooking their belts together and slipping their belts through one loop of their jeans, they were ready to climb. Jerry led the way, climbing onto the lowest limb then up into the tree branches. Then followed Sam, Joey, and Cal, with Tom bringing up the rear, each crawling and slipping over the tree trunk trying to hold onto the tree limbs. Covered with green slime and looking a bit like their heroes The Green Hornet—or maybe Batman who had been slimed—they continued the climb to reach the other side.

Just as Sam reached to help Joey off the tree, he saw a pair of eyes staring back at him. "Look over in the bushes!" said Sam, obviously startled.

"What?" yelled the boys.

"It's the eyes again," said Sam. "And something is moving this way. Hurry, get through the tree."

Higher and higher, over and under, they climbed through the tree. It was a challenge, but everyone made it breathing heavily.

"It was just an animal," said Tom when they all had their feet on solid ground. We're letting our imagination get the best of us."

"I agree," said Jerry. "Let's head toward the ship. Has anyone seen the ship yet?"

"Hold it," said Joey. "Where is the ship, Jerry? You said we would see it once we climbed over the tree that covered the mud pit. Well, where is it? There's *no ship*!"

"I am telling you it's there. I promise," said Jerry. "When I saw the ship, I was on the other side of the mud pit, not on this side. Its masts and sails came right up out of the mud pit. I swear . . . cross my heart hope to die."

"That's it, Jerry," spurted Cal. "You'll need to cross back over the tree trunk and climb into the mud pit. You must have been *in* the mud and caused the mud to move. When the mud moves, the ship moves. We'll be able to see the pirate ship when someone gets back into the mud. That's the only answer."

"I think he might be right, Jerry. You're the only one who's seen the ship. I'll go with you," said Sam. "Let's give it a try."

"Okay, I'll go back across and get in the mud pit right at the edge where I was when I saw it last. You guys wait here and watch for the ship. No need for all of us to get muddy. No telling how long it will take for the ship to rise. Okay, let's go," said Jerry.

As they crawled back across the tree, the trunk started to crack, and the whole trunk jerked down a short way toward the surface of the mud. Before either one of them knew what was happening, they were falling. Jerry landed in the mud, away from the tree, with a mighty force. Sam managed to hold tight to a limb and move himself backward along the trunk. Drawing in his breath and opening his eyes, he looked down for Jerry.

"Jerry, you okay? Hang on. I'll get us out."

Jerry was in the mud up to his waist and sinking fast. *This is it*, he thought. *I'm going under, and I'm going to die in the mud. This is the second time in my life I have been really scared. The first time was when I was face to face with a rattlesnake. I knew if I stood still and didn't move the snake might just go away. I wasn't that scared, not really. Uncle Bud taught me well. But now I'm in this mud up to my chest and I'm sinking. My legs are stuck, and I can't move my arms. This is different. The other guys think I'm so brave. If they really knew the truth! It's not me who is brave. Sam is so much braver than I am!*

Quickly, Sam reached down and grabbed the back of Jerry's shirt and started to pull. He pulled until one of Jerry's arms was free of the mud.

"Grab a hold of the tree and try to pull yourself up," said Sam. Jerry reached out and grabbed the nearest branch, but he slipped again into the mud as the branch broke off.

Sam was still hanging onto Jerry's shirt. "Hang on to me don't let go, Sam," yelled Jerry.

"I won't, I promise," ensured Sam.

Little by little, Sam pulled Jerry closer to the tree limbs, and then finally was able to haul him up onto the trunk of the tree. Once safe, they both took long breaths and laughed at each other because they were so thoroughly covered in mud.

"Thought I was a goner, Sam," said Jerry. "You saved my life, and I won't forget it."

Jerry placed his hand on Sam's shoulder to let him know they were really pals. An odd noise caused them to look out into the mud pit. They saw the mud move back and forth. Jerry stood up spitting mud out of his mouth and wiping mud out of his eyes. And there it was, *The Black Widow*.

"Sam, look there it is!" yelled Jerry as drops of mud dripped from his arm. "Turn around and look over toward the horizon." Jerry then yelled at the others to turn and look. Just as Jerry had promised, there was the pirate ship. It was true: the mud in the pit had to move for the ship to be seen.

"Hey, Sam," said Jerry, "look over behind you on the tree limb. There's another message hanging there. Grab it quick!" Reaching out, taking care not to fall into the mud, Sam grabbed the paper off the tree limb. "Got it!"

With the excitement of nearly drowning and then seeing the pirate ship, Sam stuck the message in his pocket to deal with later. At the far edge of the mud pit, the guys were jumping up and down with excitement. Sam looked at Jerry and said, "How are we going to get back across now the tree has snapped in half? There's no way over." They sat down on the only sturdy part of the tree trunk to make sure they wouldn't fall into the mud again. "We'll just have to figure it out, Sam." As he sat there thinking, Jerry suddenly noticed a rope hanging from the top of nearby tree. "Look, Sam, a rope! I didn't see it there before. We can use it to swing over to the other side."

"Do you think it will hold us?"

"Sure. I'll go first. It will be like playing Tarzan—cool, huh?" Besides, I'm bigger and if it holds me, it will hold you. When I get to the other side, I'll tie a rock to the rope and send it back over to you."

"Sounds good to me. It's a plan."

"Sam, we can do anything when we set our minds to it." Jerry climbed off the tree trunk and onto solid land. He took hold of the rope and pulled down on it to make sure the tree limb was strong enough to hold him. When he felt confident he'd be safe, he wrapped his hands around the rope, moved back a few feet, and ran as fast as he could to gain speed to jump. When he got to the edge of the mud pit, he swung with all his might, sailed over the mud, and over to the other side he went safe and sound. Tom and Cal were there to catch him when he landed.

"Tom," ordered Jerry, "Quick—get a big rock, so we can tie it to the rope and send it back to Sam."

"Aye aye, Captain Jerry," said Tom, and off he and Cal went to find the perfect rock to tie to the rope and save Sam.

Meanwhile on the other side of the mud pit, Sam sat waiting for them. He remembered the piece of paper and pulled it from his pocket. It looked very much like the other pieces of papers. Slowly he opened it. He was just about to read it when he heard something! He froze and turned to look. *Keep cool. It's just a rabbit or deer*, he told himself. He turned back around to place his attention on the note. Things were getting spooky, and he really wished the guys would hurry up. He did not like the idea of swinging across the mud pit in the dark. He turned his thoughts back to the golden piece of paper with the rib-bone strings. Turning it over, he read:

As the next to last, a new leader is born.
Truth lies in the jaws of the yak.

He took a deep breath. *Leader, jaws, truth? What does this mean?* He thought.

"The rope! Grab it, Sam!"

He reached out just in time to grab the rope before it flew out of his reach. He stuck the note back into his pocket, stepped back, took a huge leap, and over he went.

"Catch me! I'm going to fall!" Sam yelled as he neared the far edge of the mud pit. Tom, Cal, and Jerry stood ready.

Cal ordered, "One, two, three, *grab him!*" Once more, they were together and safe—and away from the eyes that seemed to be haunting them.

They patted each other on their shoulders, reassuring themselves what great pals they would be for life. The adventures they shared built within them a bond of brotherhood that would stay with them for life.

"The ship! Let's go!" cried Jerry, and they were off pretending to be pirates in search of their ship.

CHAPTER 7

B Y THE TIME they arrived at the riverbank, it was
dusk. "I think we should set up camp here," said Jerry.
With all the mud on his clothes and in his hair, he smelled
awful. He looked like a spook; just the whites of his eyes
were showing. Cleaning up in the river would be easy.

The shadows that moved in the bushes at the edge of
the clearing were creepy. They all felt that there was always
someone watching them. It would be best if they all stayed
occupied so they would not notice. They would investigate
the ship in the morning when the sun was up.

Everyone agreed and started to pitch camp Jerry gave
the orders. Tom and Cal pulled the sleeping bags from the
backpacks while Sam and Joey gathered firewood.

Once camp was set, Joey yelled, "I'm hungry."

"Me too," said Tom.

Cal, rubbing his head, said, "Now that you mention
it, my stomach is rather empty. Let's cook dogs and roast
marshmallows."

"Great, but who has the dogs?" asked Jerry as he dug
mud out of his ears.

"I do," said Tom.

"And I have the mustard and catsup," said Cal.

Always ready for dessert, Joey whipped out marshmallows, chocolate bars, and graham crackers, which surprisingly had not been crushed. Yum! They all broke off tree branches and cleaned them of dry debris, leaving the green bark showing on the branch.

"These are just right for roasting dogs," said Jerry. "They're not too dry, and the dogs won't burn. I learned that trick from Uncle Bud. Really makes the dogs roast through and through."

When the dogs were cooked, they ate until their stomachs were almost full. Soon they heard: "Any one for s'mores?" Joey opened the bag of the marshmallows, the chocolate bars and the box of graham crackers. "Grab your roasting sticks! Yum!"

While they made s'mores, they lay around the fire, keeping warm, making up pirate stories, and talking about the games they would play on the ship. It was indeed time to tell ghost stories and sing songs. No one was sleepy and it was too early for bed.

Jerry spoke up. "Does anyone remember any of the old pirate stories the old timer in town told?"

As the fire blazed and the marshmallows roasted, one by one, each boy told his story and laughed or screamed. Sam was the best at telling the stories; he could tell them just like the old timer. Some of the boys recalled stories about their friendship and how it had all begun, and those stories always made the guys laugh—especially the stories about Big Sal and her belches. She could belt it out louder than anyone. Tom got up and pretended to imitate Big Sal. Everyone laughed hard, especially when Joey farted over and over as he laughed. The boys had conquered the playground together—playing dodge ball and baseball. Pulling together was easy for them and the thing they did best. These were good guys, and they were all thankful for the friendship they shared. One by one they fell asleep and dreamed of bravery.

The sun rose early. The morning was crisp, and a slight dew covered the ground. Fog hung over the mud pit, and the smell of honeysuckle filtered through the trees. The birds were chirping, and the small ground animals were beginning to scamper from tree to rock and from rock to the ground. The fresh smell of the river permeated the air. It was going to be a glorious day for the pirates to come alive.

Jerry was the first to wake with the sun in his face. He sat up to see two birds fighting over a worm. The fire was out, but the warm cinders were keeping his feet warm. *Wow, what a night! Cal was so funny making noises with his mouth, and Joey's farting was funny too.* He was still reminiscing about the stories of the previous night and all the goings-on when Sam and Joey woke next. Joey was hungry as usual, and Sam was rubbing his eyes. Cal and Tom were the last two to awaken. They all stretched and yawned while rubbing sleep from their eyes. Licking the chocolate from the corners of their mouths just made them hungrier. Tom pulled out an apple to eat, and Cal went for the orange. Of course, Joey managed to find another Wonder Cake.

"Don't you ever get tired of eating those things?" asked Cal.

"No way. They're the best."

Cal shook his head, and Tom punched him in the arm. "Hey, what about the ship?"

Sam looked toward the mud pit, where they had last seen the ship. "It's gone!" he said. "I know it was there last night."

"Yeah," said Jerry. "It was right over there at the end of the pit, but where did it go?"

Very puzzled, Jerry and Tom took off running to the far edge of the pit to look for the ship. Sam, Joey and Cal followed right behind.

"Everyone scatter," said Jerry, "and see what you can find. Yell the secret password if you find anything. "Scat-a-butt" was their secret password. Cal could sneeze and fart at the same time, and when he did, he would make a sound that sort of sounded like "scat-a-butt." The first time he did it, the guys laughed so hard a couple of them almost peed in their pants. From that day on, scat-a-butt was their password.

"Meet back at camp in an hour," said Jerry. Off they went in different directions searching for *The Black Widow*. Sam went to the east, Joey to the north, and Cal and Tom to the south. Jerry chose the west because that was where he remembered seeing the ship. An hour went by, and no one found anything, so back to camp they all went. To everyone's surprise, there they found a table with five chairs. The table was set with milk, fruit, nuts, bread, cheese, and jelly. "Hey, there's enough food to feed an army!" said Joey. "And that is just what we are—an army of pirates!"

"Where did that come from?" asked Sam. "Just look at the size of those oranges and apples!"

Tom looked at the table with a look of amazement, "Do you suppose it's for us?" he asked.

"Must be," reasoned Joey. "Who else could it be for?" His eyes grew larger and he licked his lips. "Let's eat!" And he took a big bite from one of the juicy apples. Tom helped himself to bread and cheese.

"Wait," said Sam. "What if it's poisoned?"

Joey started spitting bites of apple onto the ground and wiping his tongue with his shirttail. Tom dropped the bread and cheese.

"Who did this?" Jerry wondered.

Joey had actually eaten several bites of apple before he had spit out the rest, so the others looked on to see what would happen to him. After several minutes, nothing happened, and the boys decided that the food must be okay. Slowly, one by one, they sat down and started eating small bites. With smiles on their faces and fruit juices running down their chins, they filled their stomachs. It just seemed the right thing to do.

"No need for all this food to go to waste," Joey reasoned as he stuffed his mouth with another piece of cheese.

The food was good, but also very mysterious. Too many questions floated in their heads as they rubbed their stomachs. Their thoughts turned back to the pieces of paper tied in rib-bone strings—who put them there and why? There was a kind of power the notes had over them. Everyone sensed it. Why would the notes burn some of them but not others? And what about all the accidents, and the strange food showing up on that table? Who was responsible for these things? Where were the boys being led?

Curious, Sam pulled his note from his pants pocket and read the words again. There were so many words the same in all the messages, yet each was different from all the others. "What do they mean?" he asked aloud.

Cal pulled his message out of his pocket. "Listen up. I'll read my message out loud. Maybe there's something here. Maybe we can figure it out."

As Cal read, the other boys pulled their messages out too. "Wait a minute," Tom said suddenly. "Each piece of paper is shaped differently! Maybe it's a clue!"

The boys became excited. Tom continued, "I have an idea. Let's put all the pieces of paper on the table. Maybe they fit together—kinda like a jigsaw puzzle. Maybe they make a map of sorts."

The boys crowded around the table. They laid all of the messages on the table and turned them this way and that to see if they fit together in any way. Slowly, a form started to take shape. Not only did they all connect, but they looked as if they had been torn from some sort of book. The messages seemed to be telling each one of them something that they should know.

In the meantime, in the bushes there were eyes still watching. "Will they save us?" came a whisper from behind a tree. "Stay hidden, don't let them see us; it's not the right moment. The time will come. Fall back and wait." Slowly the limbs on the bushes closed back together.

CHAPTER 8

EVERY SO OFTEN there would be a treasure hunters lurking in the woods looking for pirate treasure. Zang would lead them down paths unknown to them until they were lost. Sometimes he would jump out and scare 'em looking like a ghost.

It was his job to keep the ship and its cargo safe from all intruders, for he was the Guardian of all pirates, alive or dead, or who lived somewhere between the past and present. He had kept them safe for centuries, and he was good with disguises. Once he had disguised himself as a skeleton. He'd tied himself to the mast of his ship. His shaking chains and his moans convinced the intruders that he was a pirate ghost. On other occasions, he had flown through the air in the disguise of a dragon blowing fire and sweeping down on people. What fun he had! But the best disguise ever was dressing up as the old timer, sitting under the big old oak tree in town, and telling pirate stories. He loved these stories; after all, they were all about him! He would have the kids on edge of their seats with laughter, and the adults' eyes would bulge waiting for the next segment of the story to unravel. Oh, the laughter and tears he would experience . . . remembering. Yeah, telling the stories was what had kept him going from one year to the next. All the time, no one had even noticed that he never grew any older.

Now was the time. The moon was in the right place, and the stars were struck with bright light. The spirits of the pirates had found their places, each one on a point of one particular star. It was the seventh point of the star that shined brighter than the others. For it was this star that held the spirit of the original pirates—all seven of them. However, one point of the star was not shinning as brightly, and it appeared to be missing. The seventh spirit was still missing, and that was what gave off the brightness to the star the way it had appeared for centuries before, but not now. This point belonged to Zang's soul. Because he had betrayed the original seven pirates, he was not allowed to take his place in the star until he proved to the other spirits that he was deserving of his point in the star.

He had given the kids the messages . . . set the stage. Could they find their true identity? And could they find it in time—before the next phase of the moon? So much was at stake—the brotherhood of all pirates and their secrets were all tied up in the magic of the golden eggs and feathers. *I chose them well; I did,* thought Zang as he smiled his trademark crooked smile. *They are part of it all, and soon they will know the whole story . . . our story!*

The Guardian, he called himself. He had been given that name by the Winds of Time. He was stuck on the dark side of the stars between the worlds of the past and present. Only when all the original seven pirates' souls of brotherhood gathered would the secrets of the golden eggs and the feathers tied with rib-bone strings be revealed. It would be then when he would take his place at the seventh point. The original seven pirates were pure in heart and pure in mind, and this was what he had found in Sam and Joey, Tom and Cal, Jerry and, of course, best of all, in Sally. They would be friends for life. Each of them held dear all those things that the original seven pirates held dear. All had shown bravery and courage through their adventures. They had shown love for one another, clear thoughts, and honesty. And this was exactly the same as the Pirates' Code as had been told for years. Yes, they would come together all right, and free him from living between the worlds of past and present. At last he would be able to take his place and hand over the guardianship to them.

The obstacles in front of them had so far been only a few, but they had come through them all, and there would be one more to complete. He remembered the last words of the Pirate Code: "A measure of brotherhood is a measure of time, and truth is measured by time and through eternity."

When Greybellow had taken *The Black Widow*, Zang had kept the golden eggs and the feathers hidden for their safety as well as to guard their secrets of magic. Without the seven secret codes, one could not become the captain of *The Black Widow.* But Greybellow had stolen four of the golden eggs. A storm was pulled from the bottom of the seas by the gods to brew up high waves that would push *The Black Widow* to the mud pit in order to protect the golden eggs. The storm had trapped the ship, its secrets, the pirates, and Greybellow on board and would not let them go. No one would be able to leave the ship now. The storm ghosts had kept them there as prisoners. Zang needed peace and needed to return Greybellow back to the depths where he belonged. *The Black Widow* needed its true captain. The spirit of *The Black Widow* needed to be released.

Zang's punishment for letting the four golden eggs escape into the hands of Greybellow was that he must live between the past and present with no rest or peace for eternity. He had hidden the last three golden eggs in a safe place. They would be safe until the right time came. Mankind must show true brotherhood. To throw intruders off, he had hidden other golden eggs with magic light on board sunken pirate ships to keep them guessing.

He had searched for the right combination for centuries, weighing in the truths, looking at the hearts of men and the directions of their decisions. Never before had he seen such courage, respect, and loyalty for mankind . . . so much laughter and brotherhood that this group of kids had shown. Their brotherhood was true, and it would follow them forever.

The time is right, thought Zang with great excitement, *and I have done my job setting the stage. I'm ready, but what about Sally? She is the last link. Will she make it in time? Does she really have a pure, warm heart? I must find a way to get her here!*

Trying to piece the golden papers together to form a shape, like a jigsaw puzzle, became very trying. One by one, the boys moved away from the table scratching their heads and wondering if the pieces of paper really did form a puzzle or a map. Tom and Cal had been busy drawing diagrams and trying to figure out the solution to where the ship had gone. Jerry, on the other hand, felt as if something was out there controlling their every move—some sort of strong bond of something pulling them and keeping them there, not letting go. Joey had packed plenty of extra boxes of Wonder Cakes, but felt it would be best to keep them in his backpack for now. Sam found another hole in his jeans, and that made fifteen.

Each boy was keeping busy as Zang's pirates watched on from the bushes. Zang controlled the pirate souls that had been left behind and made sure they did what he said. But he did wonder if the kids would figure out the secret of the golden pieces of paper. He knew they were trying to make them into a map, and of course, a map was useless. *I know where I will be taking them*, he thought with a chuckle.

It was time for Zang to bring Sally into the picture. Just how he would do this, he was not sure, but he had to try. Last he had seen her, she was still tied to the trunk of the old oak tree. This meant he now had to pass back through time to make sure she was released and on her way. He ordered the other pirates to watch after the boys and keep them from harm while he was away.

"Beware of the captain," he warned.

CHAPTER 9

S ALLY WAS NOT one to sit back and let the boys get the best of her. Being tied to the old oak tree was not going to stop her. *Here comes Sissy!* she thought. *She'll help me!* "Hey, Sissy! Help me untie these ropes! I'm going to get those boys."

"Sally, I can't believe they did this to you!" Sissy started working at one of the knots, but was unable to untie it. "Stop wiggling!" she told Sally. "Hold still and I'll untie you."

"They think they have a secret place in the forest," sputtered Sally, "but I know all about the tree house. I've gone there many times when they weren't there. I'm going to bomb them with dog poop, bags of bird doo doo, and anything else disgusting that I can find! I'm going to scratch their eyes out! That'll teach 'em a thing or two. Thanks Sissy—see ya later!"

"Bye, Sally. Take it easy. Tell Joey I love him."

My "Sissy disguise" is one of my best yet, if I do say so myself, thought Zang.

Sally took off running toward home. The things she was going to do to those boys would go down in the record books.

At home, she changed out of her new dress and grabbed her backpack, then off she went. Faster and faster Sally rode on her bike to the edge of the forest. As she turned onto K-2 trail, she yelled, "That's it! Here I come! You are dead meat!" When Sally arrived at the tree house, no one was in sight, and it did not appear that anyone had even been there. She was only a couple of hours behind the boys, so she knew they couldn't be that far ahead. Sally climbed the ladder and walked around the tree house searching for signs of the boys. No bags, no sleeping bags, no food! No nothing! Finally, Sally realized the boys had never been to the tree house, but where were they? "If you think you can hide from me, you are sadly mistaken," she mumbled under her breath.

Through the window at the back of the tree house, she looked out into the forest where she saw something in the grass. *I need a closer look,* she thought. *Where are the binoculars? They've got to be here somewhere. There you are!* She pulled them off the nail next to the window. *Yep, just as I suspected. Silly boys can't even cover their bikes up right. But she thought it was strange that the bikes weren't on the K-2 trail. What is that on the trunk of the tree next to their bikes? It looks like a piece of paper of some sort,* but the binoculars were no help. *Better check this out*, she said to herself.

After climbing down from the tree house, she found the trail that she thought would take her to the bikes. Farther and farther she went from the tree house. It hadn't looked that far from inside the tree house, but she kept walking. Finally, she made it, and sure enough, the bikes had been covered. *Stupid boys can't even cover their bikes right. I can do better than that. I'll teach them a lesson or two.* One by one, Sally moved the bikes to another place and hid them behind a pecan tree that had markings on the trunk that looked like carved faces. *No one will see them there*, she thought, laughing to herself. *I'll cover 'em with grass and leaves. It'll look like an animal slept here. That'll teach 'em.*

After hiding the bikes, Sally snapped her fingers. *"The piece of paper! Let's see . . . where was it?* She looked around. Suddenly she saw it stuck to a branch of a tree: a golden piece of paper with rib-bone strings. *I wonder what's inside!"* She pulled the piece of paper off the tree, opened it, and read:

> The warmth of a good heart and the determination of a good soul must come together. The truth lies in the jaws of the yak.

These were strange words to write on a piece of paper and stick to a tree. *But I love the words*, thought Sally. *They make me feel good. Many of the kids at school have said that I have a warm heart. Even my teachers think I'm the most determined student in class. I need to get started if I'm going to catch up to the guys and crush them to smithereens!* As she stuck the piece of paper into her backpack and prepared to leave, she happened to look down. There on the ground was a rock formation in the shape of an arrow and, of all things, lying next to it, a Wonder Cake wrapper—with half a cake still inside!

Something's wrong, thought Sally. *Joey would never leave behind a Wonder Cake wrapper with cake still inside. It's not his nature.* She looked around and found another group of arrows made from rocks. Finding one formation of arrows after another, she followed them. *Mom use to bring me this way,* she remembered. *The trail goes to the water hole where we would swim and camp out near the Caves of Wind. That's a half-day hike. I wonder if those guys went to the water hole to camp. Or maybe to the caves, and they didn't tell anyone. It would be just like them. I know a shortcut and will make better time. I'll sneak up on 'em and scare 'em to death. They'll never expect me to show up!* Off she went, totally unaware of the adventure that was ahead of her.

The shortcut turned out to be much harder; the forest was hotter and more humid, and there were lots of trees and bushes to get through. *Mother must have used the rock formations that are shaped like arrows to follow,* Sally thought. *But I sure don't remember them.* It was a tough trail to follow, but the arrows kept her on path. She decided to rest at the caves. Inside one of the caves, she saw more Wonder Cake wrappers. She was on the right track; the boys had come this way after all.

The cave was cool and not as humid. Settling down and looking through her backpack, she found a half-eaten turkey sandwich and chomped down. *Boy does this taste good! Better rest here for a little bit.* She leaned back. Glancing up, she saw a skull and crossbones that had been etched into the rocks high in the ceiling of the cave. And there were arrows that pointed across the ceiling!

"Wow, I bet pirates stayed in here," she said out loud. "I wonder what else they hid here!" As she stood to her feet, she noticed more rib-bone strings on the ground near her backpack. *These are just like the strings tied to my note,* she thought, picking them up. *This certainly is odd.* Each rib-bone string was burned at both ends. She stuck them in her pocket thinking they would make good hair ties to hold her ponytail or pig tails when she wore them. *Think I'll check out the arrows and see where they may lead.* She loved a good puzzle, and searching for clues was right up her alley. *This sure does feel like a puzzle!*

It was hard to see deep in the dark cave, but then she remembered the tiny flashlight in her backpack. She pulled it out and flipped the switch, but the light was very dim. *Batteries must be going dead.* Shaking it to get a better light, she stumbled over something, and down she went, dropping the flashlight. When she picked it up, she just had enough light to see that she'd landed on a skeleton! The rattling of the bones scared her brainless, and she dropped the flashlight again. *Where is that flashlight?*

The wind that was blowing thru the caves sounded like human voices. The holes in the side of the cave started looking like eyes staring back at her. She was so scared she found it difficult to swallow; her mouth was dry as dirt. She thought she heard someone saying, "Save us! Save us!" coming from the back of the cave where she was headed. That did it! She grabbed her backpack, turned around, and ran fast as she could out of the cave. She ran down the trail and didn't stop until she reached the bottom where the water hole was. *Boy was that spooky! Did I really hear someone?* Walking by herself, she realized her imagination had gotten away from her. There couldn't have been voices in the cave. Down the trail she went planning how to get back at the guys. The turkey sandwich had not settled with her, and out came a belch. It was a good one. *Wonder how I do that? Think I will practice.* One after the other, she held her breath and out they came. *Really good, loud burps,* she thought. "I'll be ready to blast ya!" she yelled.

At the water hole she could see the boys had been there. One of them had left his underpants behind! She poked them with a stick. Joey's name was on the inside of the waistband. *Must be his gym pants. Uck!*

It was hot, and the cool water looked mighty inviting. She looked around. There was no one in sight. Off came the shorts, then the shirt. *After all*, she thought, *my pants and bra look like a bathing suit!* She dove into the water. She was a really good swimmer; in fact, she had won the second-place medal in the long-distance race. She was determined to beat Tom next year. *He wins every year, but not next year. I have been practicing every day at the YMCA, and I'm getting faster!* She dove down to the bottom of the spring-fed water hole and opened her eyes. The water was clear, and she could see fish swimming, darting from one place to the next. They were fun to watch. Up she went for another breath of air. This time she would swim down to the bottom. Legs kicking and arms stretching one by one, she was almost to the bottom when something grabbed her leg. Turning, she saw a shoe near her foot. The laces were wrapping themselves around her leg. *Where did the shoe come from?* she thought. Reaching out and untangling the laces, she thought, *I bet that shoe has been here floating from last year. Someone's always losing shoes and clothes here.* She looked out toward the deeper end of the water hole to see the fish swim. Needing another breath, she swam up to the top, carrying the shoe. When she reached the surface, she climbed out of the water, threw the old shoe to the bank, and didn't give it another thought. *Never know what you can find in the water hole. What fun*, she thought. *I wish Tom were here. I'd show him a thing or two about swimming.*

Time to jump off the cliff. Sally climbed up the cliffs to get to the top, then she looked around to find just the right jumping-off spot.

"What's that in the water?" she said out loud. "I don't remember seeing anything down there." When she took a second look, she thought, *Uhm, must be the shadow of the clouds.* She took a couple of steps back, then ran forward, and off she jumped. She kept her legs straight, and then her body sliced through the water without even a splash—just as straight as a knife. It was a smooth hit, and her dive coach Mr. Sims would have been proud. She hit the bottom and was about to push off when she saw two black, piercing, empty eyes staring at her. They were like black holes in rocks. She imagined that they might suck her in, and she would be doomed for life. Frightened, she tried to scream under the water. Within a split second she pushed off with her legs, swam to the surface, and scrambled out onto the shore. *Whatever it is, it's not getting me, and that's for sure!*

Tripping over her feet and gathering her things, she quickly put her shorts, shirt, and tennis shoes on and took off running. All the time she could hear strange noises behind her as she ran down the trail. Running was not her best sport. She was slow, but knew she needed to move as fast as she could. Wondering if she was being followed, she slowed down to catch her breath. As she turned around to look, she stepped behind a tree for protection. *No—no one! I'm safe. Didn't know I could run that fast! Better rest for a moment and catch my breath.* She sat down behind the tree, and before she knew it, fell asleep.

When Sally woke, the sunlight was in her eyes. Covering them with her hands, she wished she had brought her cool shades—the red shades with the pink flowers. *So cool!* Sitting up, she took an apple out of her bag and went back over what she had seen under the water. *The eyes were blacker that black,* she thought. *And they were yellow where the white should be. Was it a face or not? I can't remember. Maybe I just imagined it. Oh well, better get started. I'm getting behind.*

She looked around and discovered more arrows on surrounding tree trunks. She knew she was on the right trail. Then she saw something hanging on an arrow on a nearby tree. It looked like more rib-bone strings—two of them. *Where did they come from?* she wondered. *The boys leave things everywhere! No wonder I can follow them so easily. Lazy, that's what they are!* Removing the strings from the arrow and sticking them into her backpack, she knew exactly what she was going to do with them.

"When I catch up with those guys, I'm going to use these strings and tie all their shoes together. That'll fix them!"

But then she heard the sounds again! She jumped up and took off running. Running fast down the trail and not paying attention, she tripped over a log and fell into the edge of the mud pit. Her face hit first, and then the rest of her followed, mud flying up into the air.

"What now!" she sputtered. "Ooh, mud! Now I've done it! Just look at me!" She wiped the mud off her face and out of her mouth. "Uck! It's all over me!" she said. "How in the world did I trip over that log?" *I'm glad Cal isn't here,* she thought, *he would laugh his head off—he is so cute.* Looking at what a mess she was and feeling sorry for herself, she really did wish she was with the boys; at least she would have them to talk to instead of having to talk to herself. "They just can't be much farther."

As Sally stood up and began scrapping off the mud, she heard something in the bushes. She stopped, waited, and listened, thinking to herself, *What would Jerry do? I know he would say, "Better get across the mud pit now, worm ball!"* Wiping more mud from her face and out of her eyes, she looked up through the beams of sunlight. There in the tree she spotted a rope with a rock hanging at the end. *It's hanging too far over the mud pit, and green slime is everywhere,* she thought. *How on earth will I get it?*

At the edge of the pit was a long curved branch that had fallen from one of the black oaks. They were the strongest trees around that part of the country. She could use it to reach for the rope. It took three tries before she got it. She gathered her things and packed them into her backpack. Then she grabbed the rope, moved back as far as she could, then took off running. Lifting her legs into the air, she leaped as high as she could holding tight to the rope. Over the mud pit she went.

When she was still in midair, she heard a crack. It was the limb that her rope was tied to! Down she went back into the mud pit. This time, she landed in a deep area, and she began to sink fast. The weight of her backpack was pulling on her shoulders. She grabbed at nearby bushes, grasses, and rocks and tried to pull herself out of the mud. With hands full of grass and small branches, she was going under. *There is no hope!* she thought in desperation. *I am going to die in the mud pit!* Out of nowhere, she felt something catch the back of her bag. She struggled to escape. Then she felt something grab her shirt. *Is that a hand on my arm?* Still struggling, she felt herself yanked suddenly upward. The next thing she knew, she had been pulled to safety. Rolling over on solid ground, coughing and spitting mud, trying to speak, Sally looked around only to find no one there. She sat up and looked around again. Still no one! She yelled, "Who's there? Joey! That you?" She stood up, re-adjusted her backpack, cleaned off some of the mud, and set off at a run. She didn't look back for fear that she would see something she didn't want to see.

Zang had been hiding in the bushes watching Sally. Knowing she was not going to make it, he had reached out and grabbed her and pulled her to shore. She had fought so hard! *Just a little help never hurt anyone,* he thought. Her determination to find the boys and face the obstacles single-handedly was what made her so brave. She was the other link that closed the ring and made the adventure so interesting. *It won't be long,* Zang thought to himself. What a gal—just like her great-great-gandmama Ela. I will be free soon.

CHAPTER 10

THE EXHAUSTING EXPERIENCE in the mud pit left Sally tired and thirsty. As soon as she could, she would find a spot and sit down to rest—a safe place where she could make sure no one was following.

Finally finding a spot, she sat down and dug through her backpack for some tissues. *I always have some in here somewhere! I've got to get some of this stinky mud off me. There they are—spring flower scent—now just how did they come up with that?* Another bit of digging through the backpack and half of a package of Wonder Cakes popped out. An appetite for Wonder Cakes was the one thing she and Joey had in common. They loved them, and could eat a dozen each. Stuffing one in her mouth and chomping away, she licked the chocolate off her fingers. *How sweet it is,* she thought.

As she finished off her snack, she noticed another golden piece of paper with strings tied around it stuck under a bush. She picked it up and realized that it looked just like the one in her bag. She looked through her backpack, but hers was gone.

"Must have lost it in the mud pit," she said aloud. With little hesitation, she picked up the golden paper, removed the rib-bone string, and read:

The warmth of a good heart and the determination of a good soul must come together. Truth lies in the jaws of the yak.

"This message sounds exactly the same as the one missing from my bag!" she said aloud. *Good soul, heart and determination; what strange words to write,* she thought. *How did this get here and out of my backpack?* She looked around to find clues, but there didn't seem to be any, so she decided to put the message back into her backpack. Her thoughts turned to the boys. *I have to find them now! Too many things are happening. I'm really feeling pretty weird, and talking out loud is not cutting it!*

In the distance she could hear voices. "It sounds like Tom and Cal. Maybe they're close by." The wind picked up from nowhere. A very large limb had broken off from one the black oak trees and lay at an angle, still attached to the tree trunk.

"Maybe from up there I can see the guys. Wonder if it'll hold me," she muttered. So she began to climb. One foot in front of the other, she climbed higher and higher. When she got close to the place where the limb was still barely attached to the tree, she stood on her toes to see out.

"What a boat!" she yelled, grabbing onto a branch that was just over her head. She took another look. Well, it was a boat of sorts. She climbed higher in the tree. When she could go no farther, she held on tightly to the tree trunk and looked again for the boat. *I wonder where it went. There it is! Oh my gosh! A big boat!* Stretching even farther out, she could see a ragged flag with a skull and crossbones flying high on the mast. *A pirate ship! I wonder how it got there and whose it is.*

She stretched out a bit more and looked harder to see what was written on the side of the ship. She belched one of her biggest belches. *Boy that felt good! Happens every time I stretch. But what is that written on the side of the ship?* Squinting her eyes, she read the words: *The Black Widow.*

"What kind of boat is that?" As she pondered, low and behold, she spotted the boys. They were playing pirates, and their antics struck her funny. *That is the funniest thing I have ever seen.* They were running around using sticks like swords. Sam had tied a rag tied around his head, and it looked as if he had made a patch over one eye. Sally laughed out loud until her sides ached. Joey was pretending to be a pirate, and Tom was strutting around the deck waiving a stick like a sword. It was just too much and too funny for words.

Sally was not a small girl, and the big black oak was very old. Even with one limb down, it was an impressive tree—a large base surrounded by big roots, and branches that reached down to the ground. It was a beautiful tree. There was a large opening on the south side of the trunk caused by some sort of injury long ago. Animals used it as shelter from the weather, and from time to time the animals would hide their food there. But the old tree was not a match for the weight of Sally, who was now perched on one of the upper branches, where the new growth began. She heard an ominous crack, and then a snap, and before she knew what was happening, down she came, treetop and all. One branch at a time she fell trying to hold onto the next, legs tumbling, arms bending, and hands grabbing onto whatever was in her reach. Her hair was tangling in the leaves and twigs, and everything hurt! She screamed out loud as she fell, her mouth wide open with leaves, bark, and dirt entering and choking her scream down to a small squeal.

"Help me, I'm falling!"

The pirate fights stopped the minute the boys heard the popping, crackling, and screaming. They took off running to see who was screaming and what was falling. As they reached the damaged tree, they saw Sally all tangled with branches, leaves, and twigs. She was crying.

Tom yelled first, "Look, it's Sally!" He started pulling the branches back while Cal cleared away leaves and twigs.

Joey kept yelling, "Are you okay, Sally? Are you okay?" After a few minutes, Sally was free, and the boys pulled her out from under the tree to safety.

"Any bones broken, Sally?" asked Jerry.

"Don't touch me, you pig," yelled Sally. "Quit pulling my hair! Get off me! Yes, I'm okay." Sally stood up and brushed off her clothes and pushed her hair back as the boys looked on.

"What are you doing here, Sally? How did you ever find this place?" asked Joey.

"If you would just shut up for a minute, I'll tell you. First of all, it wasn't hard with the trail of Wonder Cake wrappers, Joey. And what is up with the skull and crossbones and arrows?"

"Seriously, Sally, how did you get here?" asked Jerry.

"I just told you how I got here, scumbag! Don't you listen? I wanted to come too, so I went to the tree house and no one was there. When I climbed up and looked out the window, I saw your bikes. It wasn't hard to figure you went into the forest."

"You found our bikes?" yelled Joey very surprised.

"Yeah, it wasn't that hard. They stuck out like a sore thumb. Besides, Mom used to bring me . . . wait a minute, why am I answering all these questions? How did *you* get here and where is that boat I saw from the top of the tree?"

"It's a ship, Sally, not a boat," stated Joey.

"Whatever."

Not sure how to answer her, all the boys looked at Jerry.

"We don't have to tell you anything, Sally, and if you're so smart, you'll just turn around and go back the same way you came," said Jerry.

"Listen here, you two-legged bull frog, I will go where I want and stay where I want. You got it, scumbag?"

As Jerry and Sally continued to argue, Joey picked up Sally's backpack and her tennis shoes and began to dust the leaves and dirt from them. As he did, out of the backpack fell a golden piece of paper like the one he and the others had found.

"Hey, everyone, stop! Look what I found!" Joey held up the golden piece of paper that was tied with the rib-bone strings.

"Give it to me, stupid," said Sally. "It's mine!"

"Where did you find that, Sally?" questioned Cal.

"I first found it near the tree where the bikes were hidden. I stuck it in my backpack. Then when I fell in the mud pit, I guess I lost it. It was the strangest thing . . . I was pulled out of the mud pit by someone who disappeared. Was that you, Joey? Or you, Tom?" The boys shook their heads and stepped back.

"So how did you find it again, Sally?" said Jerry.

"Well, along the way, I sat down to eat under the trees and I found it under a bush. That was really strange. Couldn't figure how it got there!"

"Is there anything written inside?" asked Tom?

"Yeah, but I'm not sure what it means." Sally unfolded the paper and read it out loud:

The warmth of a good heart and the determination of a good soul must come together. The truth lies in the jaws of the yak.

"Isn't that the strangest thing you ever heard?" she asked.

The boys looked at one another with astonishment.

"Should we show her?" asked Joey.

"Show me what?" asked Sally. One by one, they pulled their own messages from their pockets and read them.

"Spooky," said Jerry. "Ugh! Let's get back to the ship!"

"I saw you on the ship playing pirates. Can I play too? Come on guys, I tracked you this far all by myself. Give me a break. I can do other things too. Come on!"

"Hey, Sally, you have any Wonder Cakes?" Joey asked.

Sally rolled her eyes and said, "What'sha think?"

Joey shrugged his shoulders and said, "Just thought I'd ask"

"Of course I have some. Want one, Joey?"

Joey licked his lips and went to take one when Sam grabbed his arm, "Oh, no you don't, Sally! You are not going to win us over with Wonder Cakes. Get back, Joey!"

The guys huddled together to talk it over while Sally finished putting herself together. *Good thing I didn't break anything,* she thought as she pulled more twigs and leaves from her hair, looked for cuts and scratches, and made sure everything was where it should be.

In the huddle, hands and tongues were waggling. All did agree that she really couldn't go back. She would tell the other kids, and everyone in town. Tom brought up a point, "Look, last year in the contest for crossword puzzles and word association games she always won. She is real good at finding missing pieces of puzzles and putting things together." Cal agreed. Joey, knowing there were more Wonder Cakes, bolted out, "She can cook too! Just look at her." They all turned and looked at what a mess she was, but realized that she had made it there on her own.

"She always steps forward to defend people, doesn't she?" Cal said in her defense. "Besides, she might make a good pirate!"

Everyone agreed and decided to let her come along. There was one condition: she had to pull her own weight with no complaining or sweet talk. Sally agreed, and off to the ship they went.

"By the way, Sally, it's a *ship*, not a boat," said Sam. Away they went. "Climb aboard my mateys and lass!" Jerry said in a lowered voice.

CHAPTER 11

WHEN THEY GOT back on deck, Cal wandered off to think about his message while the others huddled around together to plan the day.

"Let's have a sword fight to the death!" Sam yelled.

"Nah—we did that before we rescued Sally." Joey shrugged.

"Rescue! I beg to differ. You never rescued me! I was fine," Sally bolted out at Joey.

"Jerry, you're the captain of this ship," said Tom. "You're the one who discovered it!"

"Ah, I'm not really the captain, but I think we should explore the ship and see what we can find," answered Jerry. "I'm still bothered about those messages. Aren't ya'll? Maybe if we do a search we'll learn why this ship is here and why we're getting these darn messages. What is up with the *yak* business?"

Tom and Cal agreed to go down below and search. Sam and Joey decided to search the stern and bow.

"Then I'll take the portside, said Jerry.

"Hey, what do I do?" asked Sally.

"You stay here on watch," said Jerry. "You never know who or what will appear or disappear. We'll take turns, and you're first, okay?" Sally smiled, stuck her chest out, and felt important. *I will not let them down.*

Tom climbed down the ladder, and Cal followed. With each step, the ladder creaked and rattled. The railing was damp and icky feeling. Both boys found themselves wiping their hands on their pants. The only light came from the trap door.

"Tom, do you see anything?" questioned Cal when they got to the bottom.

"Here's a door," said Tom. He pushed against the door with his shoulders, and it creaked open. Mud squished out the doorway. The smell was horrible! It reminded him of sweaty socks and gym lockers. "The windows are shut tight. Be careful coming down. It's dark," warned Tom.

Cal made it down the ladder, wiping the mud from the railing onto his pants. "Ohhh, what is on my feet?" he said. "We need light to search this place. Uck! A cobweb just smacked me in the face. What else is in here, Tom?"

"Don't be such a girl, Cal. Look for some kind of lamp or something to light. Do you have any matches?"

"Yeah, got matches in a box in my backpack up top," replied Cal.

Cal felt his way into the room, found a window, and propped it open. In the light that came in, he found several other windows and opened them. The musty smell was heavy in the belly of the ship, and the fresh air felt good. Cobwebs were everywhere. Looking around, the boys could see that crates and barrels had fallen to the floor. Mud and seaweed covered them. There were lots of empty, broken bottles, and the contents has spilled out of quite a few crate-sized baskets that had tumbled onto one another and landed in the floor or in the corners. Tom took the left side and Cal the right.

"Hey," said Cal, "There's an old oil lamp hanging from that post!" There were some matches in a little container tacked to the post. "Look at these matches . . . how long they are. Wonder if they still work," said Cal.

The oil was old in the lamp, but after a couple of tries with the matches, Cal succeeded in lighting it.

Holding the light high, Cal stated, "This looks like it would be the captain's quarters." A table was turned upside down, and books were scattered. The room was a mess. There was still seawater on the floor, and small crabs crawled around.

"Here are some old maps and log books showing the daily routine of the ship," said Cal. "It's written by the captain."

"I'd better go and check out the rest of the ship. Cal, you stay here and see what else you can, find and I'll be back in a few," said Tom.

"Check!"

Tom left the captain's quarters and climbed farther down into the belly of the ship. *This must be the cargo section.* He looked around for a lamp, tripped over a net that was tangled in chains and ropes. *Better find a lamp or some kind of light in a hurry or I'll probably kill myself,* he thought. On the post hung a lamp; he shook it to see if any oil was in it.

"Hey, Cal," he called up the ladder, "bring me some matches. I can't see down here."

"Here ya go. Tom," said Cal as he descended the ladder. "Not many matches left so be careful. I'm heading back up."

Tom lit the lamp on the first try and held it high. The light shone on the largest eggs he had ever seen. *Wow! Those are as big as the eggs Mrs. Mac showed us in science class! I bet they're ostrich eggs.* Each egg sat on a large piece of golden paper, tied with rib-bone string just like the notes the kids had found. He counted three eggs and one empty piece of golden paper. It was clear that a fourth egg was missing. *I wonder if this has something to do with the messages,* thought Tom. *The paper and strings are the same. Think I'd better go and get the others to see all this.*

Holding the lamp in one hand, Tom started climbing up the ladder while holding onto the slippery railing with the other hand. As he looked closer behind the ladder, something caught his eye—it was a big basket with something hanging out. He could not make it out, so he climbed back down and hung the lamp on a nail. When he bent down for a closer look, he found a locket tied to a scarf. He picked it up and opened it to find a picture of a beautiful lady. She reminded him of a family picture hanging on the wall at home. *Wonder who the lady in the locket was.* Standing up and grabbing the lamp, he shoved the locket into his pocket, and back up the ladder he went. As he climbed, the chain on the locket got hung up on a broken section of railing and slipped out of his pocket. It landed back on the floor, and Tom didn't even notice.

"Cal, you still in there?" asked Tom.

"Yeah. I found the captain's log. Guess who the captain of this ship was? Greybellow! Remember the stories the old timer in town told of Captain Greybellow? They're real stories! Just look at this stuff in this book."

"Come on. Let's get the others," said Tom.

"What did you find, Tom?"

"Better get Jerry. You won't believe what I found! Eggs—large eggs, Cal," Tom said with a look of surprise.

<hr>

Sam and Joey were still looking around the stern.

"I'm hungry," said Joey. "Wish I had a Wonder Cake." He sat down on a bucket turned upside down and wiped his lips. "Hurry up, Sam, my stomach feels like the Carlsbad Cavern—empty. Come on, Sam, there's nothing here! Let's go and get something to eat."

"Yeah," said Sam, "I can't find anything but ropes and chains. Did you find anything at all Joey?"

"Only this bucket," said Joey as he stood up. But as he stood up, his attention was diverted. "Hey . . . look, Sam," he said. "On the side of the ship . . . what does it say?"

Sam climbed over more ropes and chains to read what was carved into the wood along the inside of the railing. Squatting down and using his shirttail to wipe off some of the green slime, letter by letter, word by word, he was finally able to read:

As the next to last, a new leader is born.

Falling backward on his butt and pushing himself farther away with the heels of his feet, he could not believe what he just read. *It's the same message that was written on my note!*

"Look, Joey, read this. It's the same." Sam was shaking as he handed his golden piece of paper over to Joey.

"We need to show this to Jerry," said Joey. "Let's go."

Jerry was still searching the stern when Sam, Joey, Tom, and Cal came running. *What now?* thought Jerry. *All of them screaming at once would drive anyone crazy.*

"Quiet!" Jerry yelled. "One at a time!"

Each one, in his turn, told the others of his findings.

"Yeah, yeah, let's go check it out," Jerry said annoyed. They were walking toward the ladder when Joey saw more letters behind some ropes entangled in a sail. "Hold up a minute," he said excitedly. "Look!" He pushed the ropes aside, pulled the sail away, and wiped mud off the letters with his hands. He read:

> The awareness of six who are together will show strength in power.

Joey looked around to find Sam. "Look, Sam, it's like what you found," he said, "but it's just like the message that I found."

"Guys," said Sam, "these messages have something to do with this ship. Something tells me we will find the rest of them burned into the ship somewhere, just like these, so let's take a look."

"You might have something, Sam," said Cal, "but wait until you see what we found below in the captain's quarters. You just won't believe it!"

"Let's go down below," said Jerry. "We'll search for the messages on deck later."

Everyone climbed down the ladder and squeezed into the captain's quarters. They all stood around Cal as he picked up the log and showed everyone the entry naming Greybellow as the captain of *The Bluebird*.

"Can you believe it?" Cal said. "The old timer in town . . . his stories—they're real! It's hard to read the writing, but his book seems to be full of the coming and goings of Captain Greybellow and someone named Zang," said Cal.

"What else did you find?" asked Sam.

"Let's go down into the hull where the cargo section is, and you'll see what else we found!" blurted Tom.

Down they went, Cal holding a lamp and Tom leading the way.

⁂

The gang was down in the cargo area when Zang arrived on the ship. *So much to do to get them ready*, he thought. *Sally got here faster than I thought she would. She is really the knot that binds them together. The time is near! Better see about the eggs.* Not realizing what the boys had already found, he began his search.

⁂

Below in the cargo area, Tom showed the others the three eggs.

"Look at how big these things are!" he said with excitement. "Don't they remind you of the ostrich eggs we saw in Mrs. Macs' class?" The gang shook their heads in agreement. Each egg was sitting on golden paper with the edges torn and rib-bone strings wrapped around them.

"Cal, bring the light closer," said Tom. Do you guys have your messages?"

Joey pulled his out, spilling Wonder Cake crumbs on the decking.

"Here you go, Tom. I have mine," he said.

"Untie the strings, Joey," said Tom. "I don't want to be burned like before."

Before he could say any more, Joey unrolled the golden piece of paper. Immediately, a bright white light came from the paper as it left Joey's hands and raised itself up in the air. The boys moved back, eyes and mouths wide open with surprise. They grabbed onto each other and held on tight. The paper that had been in Joey's hand floated in midair to where the eggs lay and fit perfectly onto the edge of one of the golden papers under one of the eggs. Screaming at the top of their lungs, they all ran. Pushing and shoving, they climbed the ladder until they all were on deck. Then they jumped off the ship for safety.

"What's going on?" asked Sally.

"Run for your life!" yelled Cal.

"Run!" yelled Joey.

"Get out of here!" echoed Sam.

Cal fell on the ground out of breath, and looked back at the ship, trembling. "Did you see what I think we saw?" he cried out.

"Yeah," said Sam. "The paper really floated in the air—and made light!"

"What floated in the air?" screamed Sally as she stomped her feet. Her cheeks were turning red in exasperation!

Jerry took a deep breath and told Sally what happened.

"That's impossible," Sally argued. "Paper just doesn't light up and float in the air!"

"But it happened!" blurted Joey.

"Everyone get your messages," ordered Jerry. "Let's go back to the ship. I think we are close to the answers."

"Not me!" said Joey. "I'm not going back. That was way too weird and scary for me!"

"Come on, Joey, if we stick together, nothing can hurt us," Sam said with a reassuring smile.

"Joey, we're too powerful together," Sally said.

"Sally, you weren't there," exclaimed Joey. "It was spooky!"

Patting Joey on the shoulder, Sally reassured him that nothing was going to happen.

"But Sally," continued Joey, "It floated!"

"Joey, we'll be at your side the whole time," blurted Sam, and Cal agreed. Joey shook his head and finally indicated that he was willing to go. They all dug through their backpacks and found their messages.

"Okay—stay close and keep your eyes open," said Tom, clearly taking the lead over the others. "Let's get moving."

Jerry was first to climb the rope ladder back onto the ship, and he helped the others climb up and over the side.

When it came time to go down below, Joey squirmed around and bolted away from the others. "It's best I stay on deck. After all, someone needs to be the lookout, and it's my turn. Sally, stay with me, please!"

"No way," responded Sally. "I want to see this for myself. You sit right here, and you'll be okay."

"Fine!" said Joey. He sat on an overturned bucket near the portside holding onto the edge of a billy club rack that was fastened to the forward mast. *What happened to "we'll be at your side,"* thought Joey. Sally smiled at Joey, gave him a little wave, and headed off to join the others down below.

⚜

At the helm, Zang spotted Joey sitting on the bucket and decided it was time to make his presence known. Slowly, he moved in behind the boy and yelled, "Joey!"

Joey jumped, turned, and saw Zang. He was standing tall, dressed in black pants and a shirt half buttoned with ruffles trailing down the front. His coat was made of a heavy material with long tails hanging down. A large sword hung off his belt. He wore a big black hat with a red feather, and his long, brown hair was tied at the back of his neck with some sort of black ribbon. He was a sight to behold. Joey's heart thumped loud, a lump formed in his throat, and his mouth hung open. He didn't know whether to run or hold his stance. Without another thought, Joey felt his feet moving, and off he stumbled, down the ladder yelling for his buddies. Zang followed close behind.

Sally was the first to look up and see Joey flying down the ladder. "Look out!" she yelled. Joey fell to the floor with a huge thump, his face as white as snow.

"You look like you saw a ghost, Joey," said Sally.

Joey moved closer to Sally.

"You might just say that," he said, trembling and grabbing Sally's arm. As he did so, he was watching to see if what he had seen was coming down the ladder after him! He held onto her arm tighter.

"You're hurting me! Let go, Joey."

"You okay, Joey?" asked Sam.

"Yeah . . . yeah . . ."

Tom, Sam, and Jerry turned back to the eggs.

"Okay," ordered Tom, "everyone pull your messages and let's see if there's a connection to the eggs."

When the kids held their messages in the palms of their hands, the pieces of golden papers lit up and moved toward the eggs and took their places just as the first one had done. It was Cal and Sam's messages that floated in the air as the three eggs filled with light.

"Look, there are four more empty places where eggs used to sit," said Tom. "I saw only one empty spot before."

"Look around, everyone, and let's see if we can find more eggs," suggested Cal. But Sally found herself drawn toward the eggs that were sitting in the pockets of the golden paper. There was something magical about them. Closer to the eggs she moved. As she reached out to touch one, she saw something in the dark move. She looked around. There, at the foot of the ladder, stood Zang. Sally screamed.

"*No!* Don't touch 'em," yelled Zang, moving so that he stood between her and the eggs. Sally turned and hid behind Cal, holding onto his waist as tightly as she could.

They had never seen anyone dressed as he was dressed. He was very frightening, and there was no place to run. Tom spied a billy club and tried to grab it to defend them.

Sally yelled, "Look, you can see right through him. He's a ghost!"

Zang lowered his voice and spoke very softly. "Wait, don't be scared." He quickly changed himself into the old timer.

"Where did you come from?" asked Sally, not quite as frightened.

"You kids know who I am—the old timer from town. I see you by the big oak tree," Zang said reassuringly.

"Calm down everyone, sit on these crates, and I will tell you. My real name is Zang, and I brought you here."

"No you didn't, I got here all by myself," argued Sally.

"Quiet, now," said Zang, "and listen!"

Zang began to tell them about the magic of the eggs and the feathers, and why they were on *The Black Widow*. But most of all, he told them who he was.

CHAPTER 12

"L ONG AGO BEFORE pirates were pirates," began Zang, "they were sailors of the sea. It was their job to carry trade goods back and forth and to bring the fishes of the sea to the people of the world. They sailed their ships east and west learning of the new worlds. New goods and foods and ways of growing food were brought to the poor, and their lives improved, and the way of the world got better. They were prospering sailors. But greed soon began to show its ugly face. Sailors took money from kings to store in their treasuries. They robbed from the poor. Treaties of wealth were broken, and the killing began. The sailors turned their backs on the poor to get the gold. The people of all lands were lied to and treated badly. Their lives were taken, their souls were stifled, and their hearts had no joy. Trust and honor were gone, and only fear was left.

"Seven sailors gathered and decided to fight back. They were known as the Original Seven. They wrote a code of honor that became known as the Pirates' Code for all sailors who pirated to live by. The secrets of the shipways and passages of the deep were given only to those who took the oath and lived by it. The pirates stole from the rich and gave to the poor.

"It was during this time that the original seven made a voyage and learned of the golden eggs and their magic. It was rare birds with golden feathers that laid these eggs, and only the original seven knew of their whereabouts. Because of the good that the original seven did, they were the only ones allowed to experience the mystery of the magic golden eggs. They told no one of the magic or the whereabouts of the birds and vowed to keep the magical eggs safe from thieves. Kings and heads of countries sought these birds for their magical powers. You see, they believed they would give them eternal life and riches.

"When the time came for each of the original seven pirates to die, the birds would lay a special egg. With the help of their magic feathers, the birds would encase the soul of each pirate in an egg. The eggs were then wrapped in a gold parchment and tied with rib-bone strings. But on each parchment paper was written something of what held the seven original pirates together.

"To protect the souls of the original pirates, the birds created a special star in the heavens and sent their spirits to the star. So that sailors and pirates would recognize the star, they created seven points on the star and caused each point to shine as if it held all seven spirits. As the original pirates who lived by the pirate code died, their spirits gathered on the star and made it shine brightly.

"The golden eggs and the feathers that had protected the pirates' souls were placed on a ship, *The Black Widow,* and it too was given spirit in order to keep the eggs and feathers protected. A Guardian would guide the ship as its captain for eternity. The golden eggs, the golden feathers, and the original pirate souls were well hidden on the ship along with the Pirate Code.

"A great storm brewed one night, and as the sailors played a game of cards, the ship was completely lost along with the eggs and feathers and all their secrets. Through the course of time, the eggs and feathers were separated, and the seven-point star lost its luster. Wars between the pirates raged on and on for centuries. They no longer were men of trust, loyalty, and honor. They had become thieves in the night; they were dishonest and cheated men as well as themselves.

"All that the original pirates had been was now lost. I, the Guardian, was lost as well. I cheated the original pirates and lied to them. And it was I who lost her, *The Black Widow,* in a card game to Captain Kilo. Later, in a battle at sea, he lost the ship to Captain Greybellow, a captain of the Royal Navy. The golden eggs and feathers were seen no more, and the magic was gone.

"I have journeyed for centuries looking and listening for the true bloodlines of the original pirates. My spirit cannot go to the star in the heavens until I prove myself worthy, and people belonging to all the bloodlines of the original seven are here face to face.

"It was I who guided you to the ship and set the table with food. And now I need your help. All the stories I told . . . well, they were about me and the other pirates throughout time. Don't you see? You have known me all along for years!

"The messages were sent to you by the original pirates of *The Black Widow* and me," said Zang, coming to the end of his story. "I carved the words from the golden parchment papers onto my ship so they would not be forgotten. Not only are they part of you, but they are part of my ship—the ship that carried the souls of the original pirates as well as the magical powers of the eggs and feathers for centuries. We were to protect them. Come, let me show you where your words are burned into the ship."

Zang returned to the deck, followed by the gang. He showed them all where he had burned their messages into the sides of the ship. He pointed up the mast, and there hung the bones of a yak and the bones of Captain Greybellow. "All this is my past and my present," he told the kids, "even the stories I have told.

Sally started to cry. "I remember the love stories you told us about Captain Greybellow and Lady Kynan," she blubbered. "They always made me cry."

"We always thought the stories were too wild for truth," admitted Cal, and the other boys nodded in agreement.

"Zang," asked Cal, "if you really are the old timer from town, how did you get here and how do you do what you do?"

"First of all, yes I am he. I can do what I do only by the power of the spirits that the original pirates gave me; and I can use it only for good. When I realized I was scaring you by appearing as I really am, I was forced to appear as the old timer and explain everything to you. You see only what you want to see, Cal," explained Zang.

Tom pulled Sam aside. "This is nonsense! Whoever heard such a thing?" As they stood there next to the mast, they felt the ship move.

"The ship is moving!" yelled Sam.

"It's that time of day," said Zang, "between daylight and evening when the mist rolls in dark and green. It's then that the ship goes back to its resting place.

"Hurry, everyone, off the ship!"

As they stood on land, they watched the ship rise high above the waves of the sea and then crash into the mud pit once more. Then it disappeared.

"I need a Wonder Cake," said Joey, flustered.

"Me too," said Sally. "Now that you mention it, we haven't eaten since early morning.

"Let's eat," Joey yelled, as he turned and headed for his backpack.

"Cal, how did he do it?" asked Sam. "I mean change from one thing to the next." "He explained that it was what we wanted to see," answered Cal. "It's our belief that pirates still exist."

"Of course pirates are real! There is the code; we read it in the book.

"We have heard about the Pirate Code of Honor all our lives," said Sam. "They stick together, remember, Cal? They are the ultimate brotherhood . . . they stick together or die!"

"There is one thing more I need to tell you all," announced Zang. The kids all gathered around him. "Remember that creature in the water, Cal? The one you saw when you jumped from the cliffs?" Cal nodded.

"Ooh, I saw it too," said Sally.

"Yes," said Zang. "And some of you thought you saw things hiding in the bushes." Tom and Sam nodded. "Well, the creature is not real. I used the image to move you along. And that was me and my crew in the bushes. I had to stick around to make sure you stayed on the path, but I couldn't show myself. I'm sorry I scared you, but I had to test you. I needed to test your leadership, brotherhood, and heart. But, most of all, I needed to find out if you would stick together throughout everything. The messages you received were part of this test. They are what tied the original pirates together. I am very proud of all of you," finished Zang, "for the way you have proven yourselves. And I'm glad I was able to keep you all safe."

"Wow," said Jerry. "I feel better knowing that those things weren't real. This is all pretty amazing. He looked around at his friends to see that they all obviously felt the same way.

CHAPTER 13

"OKAY, ZANG, WE passed the test. Now what?" asked Jerry. "What is it you actually want from us?"

Zang did not seem to have to think hard to give them an answer. "I want you to help find the missing golden eggs and feathers, and then put them back in their proper places. When that is done, I can take my place with the original pirates in the Star of Pirates, and I won't have to roam the earth taking on the image of others. My ship *The Black Widow* can rest, for it will have carried the eggs, the feathers, and their secrets that lie belowdecks for centuries. The ship is tired, and so am I. The magic that holds my ship and me here has aged us both."

Zang turned, looked up, and pointed his sword. "Up there on the mast," he said, "See it? The skull of the yak. Inside is the journal that tells of the magic eggs and how to defeat Greybellow. I placed it on this ship long, long ago. When Greybellow took my ship from Captain Kilo and the yak died, he put my log in the yak's mouth and dared anyone to take it. The yak carried black magic, he did . . . sinful magic. Throughout the years, many have tried to retrieve that book, but they have lost their hands, arms, and heads for there is only one true person who can retrieve it. That person must be of warm heart and have true love for friendship. No one else can put their hands into the jaws of the yak and live to tell about it."

"There is only one person who falls into that category," said Cal. "Sally, it's you!"

"Me!" said Sally.

"Sure, Sally, it's you," agreed Joey.

"Why me?" questioned Sally.

"Look, Sally," said Cal. "I know it's been hard, always fighting, being made fun of. But through it all, you have always stood up for us. You have always proven your friendship. We know you love us—heck you would do anything . . . even belch your way through a fight! Remember when you blew the socks off Derek and Kyle?" Everyone laughed.

Sally hung her head. "I never thought I would hear any of you say that," she said softly. "You mean I really am one of you? We really are friends?" They all agreed. Sally sat up straight. "When will the ship be back?" she asked.

"I can use my special powers and call it back," said Zang, "for I am the real captain of *The Black Widow*. That will be the only chance we have. Are you ready, Sally?"

"Yes, but what do I do?" she asked, jumping to her feet.

"You must climb to the top of the mast. When you get there, you use your left hand to hold the yak's skull, then very gently, place your right hand inside to grasp the book. As you do this, lass, you must recite the Pirates' Code of Honor. If you use your left hand to retrieve the journal, the yak will come alive and eat it off. That is the curse it must follow."

"How does the Pirates' Code of Honor go?" asked Sally.

Zang stood and recited the Code: "Through the seven souls of brotherhood, we are the strength, and we are your honor that guides you. Have a warm heart and determination of mind, trust in the truth and above all, and stay together for eternity."

"Is this where all those messages come from?" questioned Sally.

"Yes, each of the original seven pirates gave honor to the Code with its words. They are the words that they lived by and put their trust in for centuries. The knowledge of the seas, their gold and treasures, as well as their souls are all held in the golden eggs. It is this that gives the Code of Honor for pirates to live by, and that is what gives strength for us to carry on. It will take all of us, the eggs, and the feathers for the magic power to work," explained Zang.

"Wait a minute!" Joey jumped up. "There are only six of us and only six messages. Who has the seventh?"

Zang stood up. "I am the seventh soul." He unbuttoned his shirt to show he wore the original skull and crossbones image on a gold medallion. "I have carried it from the beginning when the seven pirates were formed," he explained. "Each one carries this image next to his heart. The symbol locks all the pirate spirits in the stars. As long as Greybellow is on my ship, I am trapped."

With that said, Sally yelled, "Bring on the ship! I am ready!"

Zang held his gold medallion high above his head as he recited the Pirates' Code. The clouds turned dark. The wind came about and turned cold. The mist rolled in dark green and black and thick as mud. And, from inside the mist, the ship appeared once more.

"There she is!" yelled Sally. She looked up at the mast through the mist. "I've never been afraid of heights," she said, "but from here it looks like about a thousand feet! I hope I can make it."

"Want a Wonder Cake, Sally, before you start?" asked Joey.

"No, I'd better not," she said with a chuckle. "But when I get down, have the whole box ready!" She looked at everyone and became serious. "I know what I have to do, and I promise I will do my best."

"We know you will, Sally," said Jerry. "We're here for you." And each boy patted her on the back.

"Let's help her climb," said Jerry. Everyone boarded the ship and gathered around the main mast. Only then did they notice the golden pegs stuck in the mast. They might make Sally's climb easier. She stepped up and began to climb. There was green slime and mud all over the pegs, making them slippery. Each step was a near miss.

"If only I was smaller, maybe the climb would be easier," she called down.

"No, it will take all your strength to pull the journal out of the jaws, Sally," yelled Zang. "You are just right . . . yes, just the right size!"

Just as Sally took her left foot off one of the pegs, it came loose and fell to the deck. "Hold on tight!" yelled Cal. "You can do it, Sal!" yelled Joey.

Holding tight to the next peg, Sally continued to climb upward. When she was near the top, she found ropes and chains tangled and wrapped around the mast. These made the climb much harder. Holding onto a chain, she reached out for a rope. Something grabbed her hand. There on the other side of the mast, tangled up in ropes and chains, was the skeleton. *It feels alive,* she thought. *Could it possibly be*

Captain Greybellow? Sally started remembering the stories the old timer told over and over about how Captain Greybellow loved Lady Kynan and how he would not rest until he was with her again. *To have that kind of love someday . . .* Sally sighed as she looked at the skeleton.

Taking one more step, she fixed her foot on a peg to balance her weight. She reached for the skull of the yak. It was hanging nose down on the mast. It had a long muzzle of thick bone. The teeth were long and sharp and laid into one another. The eye sockets were shaped like chicken eggs. *All in all,* Sally thought, *it's bigger than the head of my dog but not as big as my cow's head. If the boys knew about her pet cow Jordan, they would laugh,* she thought. *Better get back on track and figure out how to retrieve this journal.*

Slowly and carefully, Sally reached out with her left hand and grabbed hold of the skull of the yak. With her right hand, she reached inside the mouth and grabbed the journal. She held her breath and pulled on the journal as hard as she could, but it was stuck in the jaws. *I'll have to push the jaws open to free the journal!* She wrapped one leg around the mast to give her leverage, then, using her left hand, she rattled the jaws loose as she began to recite the Pirates' Code of Honor. After each phrase, the jaws opened a little more, and it became easier to grasp the journal in her right hand.

As she tugged on the journal, Sally cut her arm on the yak's teeth. Blood rushed from the cut, dribbled down her arm and landed on the skeleton. That was all it took—the blood of a warm heart and the soul of a determined person. The skeleton moved and flesh took hold of the bones. "It's alive!" she yelled.

"*Oh my, what now*, she thought. *I'd better hold onto the journal tight and get down before* . . . It was then that Sally heard a sound that was like nothing she had never heard before—the scream of Captain Greybellow.

CHAPTER 14

THE SCREAM WAS terrifying, but what happened next was almost more than Sally could bear! First Captain Greybellow's fingers and hands moved very slowly. Then both arms. His bones crackled and his joints creaked as life re-entered them. Finally, flesh flowed over the bones, and life took the place of death.

"Holy crap!" yelled Sally, "Get me down from here!" She stuck the journal inside her shirt and flew down the mast, skipping pegs. Near the bottom, she missed a peg and fell tumbling down onto Cal, Joey, and Sam.

"Get off me, Sally!" said Joey. "You're squishing my Wonder Cakes."

"Did you see that? It moved!" yelled Sally.

"What moved?" asked Sam.

"Greybellow!" said Sally, obviously shaken. "He's alive!"

Looking up the mast at the transforming skeleton, Zang jumped in front of the kids to protect them. "What happened up there, Sally?" he asked.

"I did what you said," she answered. "I reached into the skull with my right hand, started reciting the code, and the next thing I knew that thing grabbed my arm!"

"There must be something you are leaving out," questioned Zang. "Think, Sally, think!" Zang screamed. "You've got to remember!"

Tears ran down Sally's face, and she began rubbing her arm with her hand. "I'm trying," she sobbed. "Give me a chance to think."

"Stop crying, Sally. Everything will be okay," said Tom, trying to reassure her. "What's wrong with your arm, Sally?" asked Cal.

"It hurts," she said between sniffles. "I cut it on the jaw or the teeth of the yak—I don't know which."

"Oh, no! The curse!" said Zang.

"What curse?" said Jerry.

"The blood from a person who has a warm heart and a determined soul is the only thing that can bring Captain Greybellow back from the dead!" explained Zang. "And it seems to be working."

"Now you tell me?" said Sally.

"Better wrap that arm, Sally," said Cal. "Are you sure you're okay?"

"But what about Captain Greybellow?" asked Jerry. "Is he alive now?"

Zang looked up the mast where he could see that the transformation of Captain Greybellow was almost complete.

"I wonder if he knows the magic of the golden eggs and feathers?" he muttered to himself. "Ah, I know'd he took them. Hid them he did. Thought he would take them back to the king and that would make up for things. Bah—stupid."

Finally Zang turned to the kids: "We need to protect the eggs, and I need to prepare you for things to come," he said quickly. "Let's get belowdecks—away from Greybellow."

Everyone agreed. When they were assembled near the golden eggs, Jerry said, "The remaining eggs need to be in a safer place. Start looking for a box or something to put them in." In the cargo hull there were many crates and barrels, but they were all too damaged to be used.

"I have a place we can hide the eggs," stated Tom. "There's a basket there behind the ladder. It would be a perfect place to hide the eggs. And there's a scarf we can use to protect them."

They all got to work. Soon they had packed all the eggs carefully inside the basket and pushed it back in place behind the ladder. All agreed it was the right place. During the process, the locket that had fallen from Toms pocket somehow managed to be dragged back into the crate, but no one even noticed it was there. When the job was done, they all prepared to leave. Cal led the way toward the ladder, but he stopped in his tracks because Captain Greybellow stood at the bottom of the ladder.

"Aye, Zang," bolted Captain Greybellow. "I see ye're still here on my ship."

"Ya, I'm still here, Captain, waiting to send you back to the depths of the sea where you belong and take my ship back," replied Zang.

Looking out his one good eye, the captain questioned, "And who may these lads and lass be?"

"By their actions, you will return to the sea," said Zang.

"Humph! Maybe. Maybe not, my friend."

Captain Greybellow moved among the lads and lass looking at each of them and sizing them up. Tom moved closer to Cal, and Sally hung onto Cal's arm while Sam and Joey stood nearby.

Jerry jumped out and yelled; "We're the defenders of the truth, and you will not harm us!" Greybellow jerked around, drew his sword, and put his face in front of Jerry's face.

There they stood, face to face, ready for a fight when Tom pulled Jerry back and said, "Let's go, guys. He's not worth it."

"Go, ya say," yelled Greybellow. "No one is going anywhere until I say you can go!" And he flew up to the top of the ladder and slammed shut the hatch. Then he disappeared into the captain's quarters. Tom scurried up and tried to open the hatch, but it was locked. "Let us out of here!" And some of the others began yelling as well.

"Be *quiet!*" yelled Tom. "Okay, Zang, it's your turn. What happens now?"

"Stand back," said Zang. He closed his eyes, held his gold medallion above his head, and recited the Pirates' Code once more. Before everyone's eyes, the hatch blew open. "Now run, lads—and lass—quickly up the ladder before he returns!"

Sally was the last one to go up. As she began to climb, she remembered the basket of eggs. *I can't leave them down here*, she thought. *I have to protect them with my life. It is just the right thing to do. I just know it is.* She climbed back down to retrieve them. Planning to pick them up and lay them on the scarf from the basket, she turned toward the ladder to make sure no one was watching, but it was too late. There in front of her stood Captain Greybellow.

"Where do ya think ye're going, my pretty?" snarled Captain Greybellow, grabbing her arm and keeping her from moving.

Sally stared back at him. "Take your boney hands off me or else!" she said. Greybellow pulled her closer to him. There was only one thing left for Sally to do. Inhaling air in her lungs, she let him have it. Out came the belch of her life. The air blew right through him to her surprise, so once more she inhaled and out it came again.

Greybellow tried to fight back by waving his hands and hat. Sally scooped the eggs in the scarf, tied it around her waist, and made a run for it. Hand over hand up the ladder she went slamming the door behind her. But, to her surprise, there he stood again right in front of her on the deck. Cal sneaked up behind Sally, untied the scarf, and handed it off to Tom. Then he grabbed Sally. Sally screamed but quickly realized it was Cal trying to help her.

"He isn't going to hurt you as long as I'm around, Sally," said Cal standing between Sally and the captain. Sally was surprised, stunned, and scared. Being protected by Cal was the greatest thing ever. The bravery of the boys frustrated Greybellow, and he disappeared.

"In here," yelled Zang from the captain's quarters.

They all ran up the ladder again and ran into the captain's quarters. Slamming the door shut, they thought they would be safe. Zang braced the door with a pair of leg bones and a skull that he found on the floor. "He can't pass through the door or walls when crossbones and a skull are placed in this way," Zang told the kids. "We're safe for now, but he is much too quiet. I wonder what he is up too."

Scratching his head, Jerry said, "Maybe we should read the captain's journal or logs. "Maybe we could learn more about the eggs and Greybellow."

Zang agreed. *But I know how the magic works*, he thought, *and it will not last for long! The log should keep them busy until Greybellow's next move.*

"The ship will go back to the mud pit along with Greybellow," Zang told the kids. "We don't have long since I was the one who called the ship forward. Sally, you were brave back there and did a good job rescuing the eggs," He turned and spoke to all of them, then focused on Sally. "Stick together you did, but, Sally, there's something about you that Greybellow likes," warned Zang. Be careful. He can be tricky."

CHAPTER 15

AFTER LEAVING THE ship, they gathered around the table near the edge of the mud pit to watch the mystery of the ship's log unravel.

"Look," said Tom, as he read the log. "Here it says the only time a pirate's spirit can make it to the Star of Pirate Souls is when the seven eggs are together forming a star. This only occurs in the seventh year, the seventh month, the seventh day, at seven minutes past the seventh hour of the morning. That's heck of a long time."

"The seventh day of the seventh month is tomorrow!" stated Jerry.

"That was quick, Jerry," said Tom. "How did you know that?"

"That's my birthday!" replied Jerry surprisingly.

"Um, weird," said Tom. "But listen to the rest: 'Each egg carries the soul of one of the original pirates. In order for the magic to work, each egg must be held by one of the original pirates or his blood kinsman. If one is missing, it won't work.'"

"Wow, I wonder if that's us?" questioned Joey.

"'If the eggs are held in the wrong hands,'" continued Jerry, "'the pirate souls will float through eternity.'"

"So that's why you are still here, Zang?" questioned Sally with empathy.

"Yes, when the four eggs went missing and Captain Greybellow had my ship, none of us could return. Over two centuries have gone by, and we have waited and waited. Then you came along."

"But you said you were the seventh original pirate," said Cal.

"Aye, I am—the last of the seven original pirates. It ends with me."

"No more real pirates, just thieves. What's the difference?" asked Joey.

"The original seven were men of honor, soul, determination, and brotherhood," explained Zang. "They were full of the love of mankind. The people of all countries had high moral values. They cared for one another and they helped one another—until the lies came. Remember when I told you how it all began? We formed a pack when there were seven of us: Maurice, Sandy, Poppy, Murdie, Mama Ela, Thomas, and me. We gave the name "pirate" to our cause so when that word was used, people would know we could be trusted. The name pirate became known to all as "People Trust for One Another." Zang took a deep breath before he continued. "Sadly, though, Thomas was shot by the king. Aye, he became the first spirit in the star, bless him."

"So are you saying that each of us came from one of those pirates on our family tree?" asked Cal.

"Aye," said Zang. "Each of you is descended from one of the original pirates. Sally, you came from the only female pirate. Mama Ela was a wonderful, warm-hearted woman. You inherited her famous belch."

"Really!" answered Sally with a big smile on her face.

"Aye, really," said Zang.

"How do you know we are their kinsman?" asked Tom.

"I know everything—how and when each of your ancestors was born and died. It is my job to know. I owe you no more than that."

"You don't have to get huffy about it," said Joey.

"Be quiet, Joey," said Jerry. "Zang, we understand that the eggs and the feathers work magic when they are together. We understand you found us and brought us here. But just how do you expect us to find the missing four eggs?"

"That is where your expert knowledge of the forest comes in, Jerry," explained Zang. "Captain Greybellow sailed *The Black Widow* all over the seas. She was picked up by the stormy mist that landed her here in the mud pit. But before that time, Greybellow must have used much of this area for a hideout. And my guess is that he hid the eggs somewhere nearby. Jerry, you acquired the skills of the forest and animals from your great-great-grandfather, and it's those skills that have gotten ya this far."

"I thought Greybellow was in the Royal Navy," blurted Sam. "So how could he have stolen the eggs? And prey tell, how did he land here of all places?"

"Aye, he was in the Royal Navy, Sam, until he found my ship and took it. Remember I told the story about how he found his beloved, dead, in the straw crate? Well, Greybellow always believed I was the one who sunk her ship, but it was Captain Kilo, not I. The treasure and Lady Kynan were onboard *The Black Widow*. Kilo was after it all—all for himself, black-hearted pirate that he was. When Greybellow boarded the ship, he did not find Kilo on board. The coward had sneaked off in a boat. Greybellow did find the treasure, and he found what was left of poor Lady Kynan. I was not on my ship, but on another preparing to fight to the death with Kilo. Truth about Lady Kynan's death sent Greybellow over the edge. I swear it's the truth."

"That's a lot for us to take in, Zang, don't you think?" questioned Jerry.

"Maybe so, matey, but ya can find the truth in my journal," stated Zang.

"You are very confusing," Sally stated shaking her head. "We've heard that old story a dozen times, and each time it changes."

"Well, my story is the truth, lass, just like the journal says."

Jerry sat back and began to think about all the adventures he'd had with his uncle, and all the lessons his uncle had taught him. He always said, "Just look at the clues that are in front of you and you can find what others cannot see." He remembered some of the stories Zang—as the old timer, or *whoever* he was—told. "That's it!" he yelled. "Tom, Cal, come with me," he called out to his friends. "Joey, Sam, and Sally stay here and help Zang."

As Tom and Cal ran off, Tom yelled, "What? Where are we going?"

⁂

Sally pulled Zang off to the side. "I want to know more about my great-great-great grandmother . . . or however many 'greats' it would be?" she asked him. "What was her name? What kind of adventures did she have?"

"We called her Mama Ela," Zang stated with pride. As Zang started to tell her stories of Mama Ela, Sally started to daydream about Greybellow. As she listened, she felt a connection to him. *He probably was married to one of the daughters of Mama Ela or maybe Lady Kynan after all,* she thought. *I feel as if I have known him all my life. Zang said I looked like her—or was it Lady Kynan? No wonder he looks at me so hard, I must look like one of 'em! I wonder if Zang was Mama Ela's husband.*

The ship was still in the mud, and Sally wanted to talk to Greybellow. Zang had finished his stories and had drifted to sleep. Slowly Sally worked her way back to the ship. She climbed up the side and onto the deck. There was a strange sensation of Greybellow's presence as she walked around the deck.

"Are you there, Captain? Are you there?" Right through the wall of the captain's quarters came a strapping figure of a man. *Wow, he was handsome,* she thought. *He must be an old man, but he doesn't really look old.* He moved toward her. He was wearing a large hat, boots to his knees, and a white flowing shirt under a red, long-tailed jacket.

"I see you've returned, lass. The sea air is quite remarkable this time of year. I love the smell of the sea. When the mist from her waves is in my face, I can hear her calling my name . . . beckoning me." Before she knew it, he jerked around and asked harshly, "Where are the eggs? You little fools, don't you know that you can't hide them from me?"

She knew he had been trying to catch her off guard. "I don't have your silly old eggs, and I don't smell any sea air, either."

"Don't mumble, girl! Speak up!"

"I don't have your fool eggs!"

"Then where are they?" he bellowed.

"Beats me! Why are you screaming at me? I'm right here," said Sally.

He stepped closer and peered into her face. "You look familiar," he said. "Do I know you?"

Backing up, she said, "No, but you might remember a relative of mine. At least I *think* she was a relative."

"And who might that be?"

In a very small voice, she squeaked out, "Kynan."

"Who'd you say?"

Rising to her feet, placing her hands on her hips, and speaking up with vigor she yelled, "*Kynan!*"

Pulling back, the captain bent from his waist and took a very hard look at Sally.

"By whippersnapper!" he said. "That's it! You do look like her. Aye, you do look like the Lady Kynan." With a look of sadness on his face, he turned and disappeared into the walls again.

"Wait!" Sally yelled, "Come back! Come back, please! I don't really look like her! I look like Mama Ela." She suddenly felt very sad for Captain Greybellow.

Tom, Cal, and Jerry arrived at the Caves of Wind.

"What are we doing here?" asked Cal as they ran into the caves.

"I don't know how," answered Jerry. "But I know this cave is a place where Greybellow or other pirates probably would hide their treasures. It's all the drawings on the walls, remember? We've got to hurry—my gut feeling tells me we haven't got long. Something horrible is going to happen if we don't find those eggs!" They came to a place in the cave where it became divided into three separate tunnels. "Tom, you go that way," ordered Jerry, pointing to his left. "Look for unusual cracks and rocks that shouldn't be there ... things that don't look like part of the natural rock formations. Remember your science classes. Cal, you go that direction and do the same. Yell out our secret password if you find anything. I'm going this way." Each one took off in a separate direction.

It was Cal who first found a tree growing out of a rock formation under an opening in the roof of the cave that let in the daylight. It looked unusual to him. He dug and pulled some of the brush out from around the tree and stood back. *This is the strangest tree to be stuck in a place like a cave,* he thought. Then it hit him. "It's a Joshua Tree!" He remembered the tree from one of the stories that Zang had told. *Why would it be here of all places. I thought they grew in the desert. I bet the pirates put it here. But why would they put it here?* He continued his search with all kinds of questions going through his head.

Tom was looking up and down the walls of the cave wiping sand out of his eyes when he saw it. Up high above him was a hole in the rock wall. Streaks of bright light shone through the hole. *Is the light a reflection of something?* he wondered. He decided to climb to the top of the rocks and investigate. At first the rocks were solid, and the climb was easy, but it wasn't long before the rocks became smaller and green slime was everywhere. He took a step and slipped. *Better hold on much tighter before I fall all the way down. Why is there green slime up this high? In science we learned slime only grows where it's wet, and the wind should keep everything dry up here.*

Higher he climbed holding onto rocks, dirt, vines, and anything else he could get his hands on. Stopping to look up, he could see the opening. *Not far to go now.* When he finally reached the opening, the light was terribly bright, making it difficult to see. Covering his eyes with his arm, he peeked out at the light. There was something about it that reminded him of the golden papers when they floated in the air. *This must be the place!* He got down on his knees where the light was not so bad and focused on crawling toward the large opening. When he had crawled only a few feet, he started falling through a hole. Rolling, tumbling, and flipping, he went down until he landed on his stomach. *Must have fallen ten feet or so,* he thought as he rolled over, sat up, and tried to shake off the surprise and pain. Still rubbing the dirt off his face, he opened his eyes. There they sat: two eggs on golden paper.

"I found them!" he screamed. "Do I dare touch 'em?" Reaching out with the palm of his hand, he touched the nearest one. It slid into his hand easily. When he tried to pick up the other one, however, it would not budge.

I've got to go get the guys! he thought. *Jerry was right the eggs were here. Just like his Uncle Bud said—look for the clues in front of you.* Carefully he placed the egg back on the golden paper for safety.

"I've got to get out of here and get help!" The wall was steep to climb. Reaching for a ledge, he fell back down. It was clear the climb would not be easy. In fact, it would be very hard. He tried repeatedly, but each time he took a step, he fell back down. It was impossible to get out. "How am I going to do this?" he asked himself. "I've got to think like Jerry!"

Jerry, on the other hand, while exploring his area of the caves, found himself in wet, marshy mud. It was sticky and thick and reminded him of crude oil. Taking his backpack off, he remembered that his small flashlight might be in the inside the pocket of his backpack. *There it is! Forgot it was there!* Shinning his flashlight on the wall, he saw carved arrows—one after another. He followed them, but it didn't take long before he was going in circles. When he finally looked down, he saw footsteps in the mud. *Are those my footsteps? Or someone else's?*

There was a light coming from an opening above a large boulder toward the end of the cave. As he walked closer, he shined his light on the wall and discovered something etched in the wall above the opening. *I need to climb a little higher to see.* Holding onto a ledge and stretching his neck, he recognized the etching as the face of an Indian Warrior. *Uncle Bud was right! Even the Indians used these caves. No wonder all the arrows are carved in the walls.* Facing the Indian warrior was another face; it looked like Zang. He remembered what Zang had told him, "Sometimes you see what you want to see." Climbing over each rock, he began to feel his way to the opening. That's when he heard a sound. He stuck his head through the opening and shined his light straight up. He was still inside the cave, but there was an opening at the top that allowed sunlight to penetrate. "Now how on earth did a tree get here?" *It's the largest tree I have ever seen!* As he marveled at the sight of the tree, he heard a sound . . . almost like someone talking. He climbed farther into the opening, and the sound got louder. It sounded like a voice he knew. His light caught something moving—was that Cal?

"Hey, Cal, you up there?"

"Jerry, that you?"

"Yeah! How did you get up there?"

"I climbed," said Cal. "Look behind the tree. There's a hole with a bright light coming through. Follow it. Climb up, but be careful. It's a tight climb and there are thorns on the tree."

"Okay. I'll be up in a few."

Jerry climbed through the back branches and headed for the top of the tree and the hole through which the light was shining so brightly.

"Wait for me, Cal," he yelled. When he finally caught up to Cal, Jerry found the light too bright to look at. "How can you see anything? It's so bright!"

"Yeah, crazy, huh?"

The light was so bright, they had to shade their eyes with a couple of old bandannas from Cal's backpack, but the light still made it difficult to see. Crawling over rocks and pebbles, they moved from the entrance farther into the cave. The trail took a sharp turn downwards. Cal first, then Tom, down they went rolling and tumbling, landing in a pool of water.

"Are you okay, Cal?" asked Jerry. "That was a sharp turn and drop!"

"Yeah, I'm okay. What about you?"

"Little bruised and wet, but I'm—oh my gosh! Look Cal!" Jerry had spotted two eggs on the ledge, sitting on golden paper and shining in the light.

"Yeah, we found the eggs! What do ya think about that, Jer? They really are here, just like you said. Should we try and pick 'em up? Look how big they are!"

"Take it easy, Cal. We don't know anything about them, not really. They could burn our hands like the messages did, remember?"

Slowly, and very carefully, Jerry touched one of the eggs. When it didn't burn him, he picked it up. Cal followed and picked up the other one. "How are we going to get 'em out of here?" asked Cal.

"We'll make bags out of our shirts and lower them down the tree one by one," Jerry said.

"Good idea, Jerry, but how are we getting up there?" Cal pointed toward the slanted tunnel they had tumbled down.

"Heck, I can't do everything, Cal! Go check for another opening in back of the cave and see if there is another way out. I'll make the bags and try to think of something."

"Okay, don't get your dander up, Jerry. If I find anything, I'll yell the secret password, okay?"

Picking up his dirty backpack, Cal could not understand why Jerry would send him to check the cave out. *He's better at this kind of thing than I am.* "Let's see, what would Tom do. He would stand up tall and walk straight in a line right into the tunnel without a thought," Cal said out loud. *Before I fall down another hole, think I'd better see if my superhero flashlight is still in my backpack from the last campout. Don't know why we didn't use them when we were on the ship or in the cave.* He found his flashlight, held it up to his face, and turned it on. *What'sha know? It works! Now I can see where I am going.* Moving slowly and listening to every sound, he examined the cave. *What's that?* He stopped in his tracks dead cold. He heard a familiar voice. Turning to his right in the tunnel, he could see more light coming from the tunnels. *Did I go in a circle? That sound was Tom's voice. It was coming from another part of the cave.*

"Tom, is that you?" he yelled with his hands cupped to make the sound travel farther.

"Yeah, where are you?" yelled Tom.

"I'm coming! How did you get here?"

"Never mind that, Cal. You won't believe what I found! Come over here and look. Be careful of the light. It's very bright."

Tom turned his flashlight off to save the batteries, and then, to Cal's surprise, he led him to more eggs. They were sitting on golden paper just like the other eggs.

"This is so cool. Jerry found more eggs back over in another part of the cave," he told Tom.

"Cal, how did you find the cave?"

"I climbed a Joshua tree to get to the opening of the tunnel and followed the light. Isn't that odd? A Joshua tree. Don't they grow in the desert? Do you think the Indians or pirates put it here? Anyway, when I got to the opening of the cave, I followed a path toward the tunnel, when I heard Jerry yell. When he climbed up the tree and joined me, we crawled along the tunnel trying to follow the light, but we slid down a hole and landed right on our butts in a pool of water.

"Where is Jerry now?"

"He is on the other side of the cave with the eggs," said Cal

"So you're both okay?"

"Yeah, we're sore and wet, but okay."

"Let's gather the eggs and head back to where Jerry is," said Tom. "Be careful picking them up. Use your shirt. Hey, where's your shirt? We'll have to make do with mine."

Scratching his belly, Cal said, "Tom is using my shirt to carry one of the eggs in."

Jerry was happy to see Cal and to learn that Tom was with him. Seeing they had the other eggs made him feel that all the lessons that his uncle had taught him had paid off. Now they just had to figure a way out of the cave, back down the tree, and to the ship. The ledge was too high above their heads. The fear of breaking the eggs was weighing heavily on his mind. Using the backpacks was out of the question—the stuff inside was too useful to leave behind.

Two eggs were cradled in bags made from his shirt and Cal's shirt. With only Tom's shirt left and more eggs, what could they do? Cal and Tom had managed to bring their eggs in Tom's shirt, but Jerry was amazed they had not broken. The boys needed to figure out a safer way to carry the eggs.

Tom came up with the idea. "Instead of using our shirts, let's use a pair of jeans. We could put two eggs in each leg and tie a knot between each one and another knot at the bottom to keep them from falling out."

Cal and Jerry looked at each other. "That's a really good idea," said Cal.

"Yeah, good work, Tom," said Jerry.

Cal spoke up. "I suggest we use my jeans since there are no holes in the legs. Both of you have holes in your jeans. Besides I still have my shorts on underneath."

With that said, Cal took his jeans off. Jerry and Tom put one egg into one of the legs and tied a knot to secure it, then the second egg, secured with a second knot. The eggs would be safe. They secured the second two eggs in the other leg of the jeans, and now they were ready to climb.

"Now let's get out of here," Jerry said. "Wait! I have an idea! Let's make a human chain. All we have to do is stand on each other's shoulders. Tom is the strongest. He can be on the bottom, then I could climb onto his shoulders holding on to the rocks of the wall. Cal, you're the lightest, you climb last and carry the eggs to the top. Once you're up on the ledge, you can help pull us up."

Tom and Cal agreed. Cal hung the jeans around his neck like a harness, with both legs hanging down in back. They were now ready.

Tom found rocks to help support his feet. When he was ready, Jerry climbed up onto his shoulders, supporting himself against several rocks. Finally, Cal began his climb. He was almost up on Jerry's shoulders when Tom yelled, "Stop! One of the eggs is slipping! The knot's coming undone! Hold still!" Tom retied the jeans leg. "There," he said, out of breath, "it won't fall out now, but climb fast."

Once Cal made it to the top of the ledge and into the tunnel, he placed the eggs on the ground in a safe place. He was so proud of himself. He decided he needed some extra help to get Tom and Jerry back up onto the ledge. He took the eggs out of the jean legs and carefully laid them back on their golden papers on the ground. Then he tied the jeans together leaving the knots in the legs, which would make it easier to climb. But now the jeans were too short, so he threaded his belt through the belt holes and buckled the buckle. Then he pitched it over the side.

"Jerry!" he yelled. "Grab the belt."

"Got it."

"Quick! Put your head through the loop get the belt under your armpits. It'll help support you."

"Okay, Tom climb," Jerry yelled. With Jerry holding onto Tom's legs, Cal leaned over the edge and held onto the jeans with all his might.

Tom grabbed hold of the belt, then the jeans legs and pulled himself up on top of the ledge. He made it.

"Okay, your turn buddy," yelled Cal.

Cal and Tom pulled on the legs of the jeans at each knot until Jerry was up on the ledge and was safe.

"That was awesome!" Jerry declared. "But we'd better get out of here in a hurry."

They packed the eggs back into the jeans, then carefully carried them back through the tunnel and down the tree. Soon they were on their way back to the ship, with triumphant smiles on their faces.

CHAPTER 16

S ALLY AND JOEY were eating Wonder Cakes and trying to explain to Zang how great they were when the boys showed up with the eggs.

"Wow—where did you find them?" asked Joey. "And where are your jeans?"

"They were in the Caves of Wind," said Tom.

"How did you know they would be there?" asked Sally.

"I remembered one of the stories Zang told us in town when he pretended to be the old timer. It was about treasures hidden in the cave where wind blew through tunnels. That was when it came to me—the eggs had to be in the Caves of Wind," explained Jerry.

"Yeah, but there are a lot of caves around here with tunnels and lots of wind," said Joey acting very suspicious.

"I just figured, if the eggs were hidden, that's where they would be. Remember when we had a scavenger hunt last summer? We found a lot of Indian arrowheads in the caves, and other explorers have found Spanish treasure. Indians and pirates used these caves to bury and hide their goods. The entrances were covered with thick brush and rocks and were well hidden. When the park rangers found the caves, they cleaned the entrances. Remember the time that forest ranger found boxes of bootleg booze from the 1920s? Well, I just followed my instincts!"

"That was very clever work, Jerry," said Zang. "How many did you find?"

"We found four eggs. That's how many were missing, wasn't it Zang?" Cal jumped in. "I'm cold. Give me my jeans." Undoing the knots and laying the eggs on the ground, the boys retrieved their jeans.

"Sally, where did ya put the other eggs?" questioned Zang.

"They're in a safe place," she said, "and I am the only one who knows where they are." Sally stood with her shoulders back, obviously feeling very proud of herself for protecting the eggs.

"We have only a few hours left before it's time," said Zang very nervously. "The eggs have to be together, Sally, or I am stuck here. Where are they?"

"Okay. Okay. I'll show you! I sunk them in the mud."

"You did *what!*" screamed Zang.

"What a great idea!" said Cal.

"I hope the mud didn't crack 'em," mumbled Zang. He was walking in circles rubbing his head, and he had a worried look on his face. "We need to get 'em now before the captain shows up again," he said, turning to Sally. "He can appear anytime he wants."

"Follow me and I'll take you to where the eggs are hidden," grumbled Sally.

High in a tree set Captain Greybellow just listening and waiting, for he knew his time was near. He also knew that the eggs the kids had found were not the real eggs. Zang would not have hidden the real eggs in a cave for others to find. But Zang had done a good job of laying treasure around the cave to fend off the intruders. It was very clever of that boy. *He has good reasoning skills*, thought Greybellow, thinking of the wall markings and the treasures that were found by the rangers! *Works well with the other boys, too. But that stuff about Sally's past and the original seven is scuff! With the real eggs, Zang can bring his crew back and sail the seas, but only if they find the feathers too. All that stuff about the pirate spirits in the stars . . . Baugh!* The captain climbed down from the tree and followed them.

"Wait!" said Zang. "Someone is following us!" Zang had a way of knowing—just as Sally did—when someone was around. "Be careful," he warned, "the captain could be near."

Arriving at the edge of the mud pit, Sally started to reach out into the mud where the eggs were hidden. But Zang yelled, "*Stop!* Don't go any further. Jerry stand here. Cal and Tom, you two walk over behind those rocks. Sam, Joey, you go on the other side of the trees. Cal, come with me behind the bushes." He pointed out to the kids where he wanted them to go. "The captain is near, and we need to separate," he said. "Go slowly, Sally, go very slowly."

Sally stood raising her eyebrows and looking very brave. "If we aren't together, he can't do anything. He doesn't have the power when we are apart, right Zang?"

Now allowing himself to be seen, Greybellow moved slowly behind Sally as she pretended to pull the eggs from under the muddy water.

"Sally . . ." Greybellow spoke softly.

Sally turned and fell backward into the muddy water. "You scared me! Now look what you've done. Where did you come from anyhow? Help me out of here!"

"Give me the eggs, lass."

"I don't have your old eggs," she said as she tried to stand up and get out of the muddy water.

"Where did you hide 'em then?" Greybellow pulled his sword from its sheath and lunged toward Sally. Zang and Cal jumped from behind the bushes and stepped out in front her.

"You are not going to hurt her!" screamed Cal as he tried to tackle the captain. Zang pulled his gold medallion out and held it high in front of Greybellow. Jerry came from behind and hit the captain behind his knees. Sam went for the sword, and Joey picked up a rock ready to strike and strike hard.

"Stop everyone!" yelled Zang. "Don't ya see, Captain? It's time. They are real, and they will set us free."

"Set us free, from what, Zang? I have been here for centuries fighting and missing you each time. Really, the only thing I'm ready to do is find the murderer of Lady Kynan and the thieves who sunk my ship. It is those who caused my pain, and I will kill anyone who gets in my way—even you, if he be you!"

"What does it take, Greybellow? I have . . ." And the arguing back and forth between them continued.

Finally Greybellow yelled, "All right—you say these lads and lass are real and that they are the kinsman of the original pirates. You say we have only a short while before we lose our chance forever. I will tell you this, Zang, if you do not speak the truth, with my last breath I will run my sword right through you, and them too!"

Zang knew the lads and lass had proven themselves very well. "You will see, Greybellow, you will see," Zang replied very cautiously.

Tom and Cal moved closer to Sam and Joey. Jerry helped Sally up, and they stood together.

"We know who we are," Jerry screamed. "We know where we came from and who we came from. But do you know, Greybellow? Do you really know who we are?"

"Yeah," yelled Joey with chocolate icing on his face. "We are the sons and daughter of the original pirates!"

"It's Mama Ela you're really scared of," said Sally.

"Yeah," the boys yelled shaking their arms and fists.

Captain Greybellow stared hard at Sally. "Be very careful, my pretty," he warned. "Be very carful, for the other pirates will eat you alive!"

"Stop trying to scare Sally," Cal warned. "She can take you out with no effort at all!"

"We are more powerful," Tom said standing with his hands on his hips for reassurance. "We stand together for what we believe in, and we believe in the Pirates' Code of Honor."

"So you think you know about the Pirates' Code of Honor?" said Greybellow with a sneer. "But do you really know about the magic of the eggs. It sounds to me like you've already figured it out, thanks to Zang."

"How do you know of these things, Greybellow?" questioned Zang.

"I know more than you think I know," stated Greybellow as he turned to the lads and lass. "Now listen up! There are three parts to the magic. The first part is that you must be kinsmen to the original pirates, and we know that you have met that requirement. The second part is that you must possess brotherhood among you. You must demonstrate honor with the spirit and soul of the original seven. You have shown that through your journey here. The third part . . ." Greybellow sniggered. "Zang did not tell you everything, did you, Zang? *The Black Widow* and her true captain must be reunited and everything must be put back the way it was before the eggs were stolen. The curse must be broken, and the truth must be told. No secrets or lies can be left behind," warned Greybellow.

"How do we do that?" asked Tom as he turned and eyed Zang, now knowing that the pirate had not told them the whole truth.

"The final truth," said Greybellow as he hung his head, "is that I too must go back and show my king that I was an honorable man and not a thief of the night. Lady Kynan of the Wetlands must be found, for she carries my heart, and without my love for her and my country, I go nowhere but on this ship. Don't believe all that Zang has told you!"

Zang explained. "The eggs carry the secrets of the past and the present. It is those powers that will allow us to prove ourselves. The eggs will tell how and why I lost my ship. They will reveal I was not a thief, but a true pirate with heart and honor according to the Pirates' Code of Honor. Even Greybellow does not know how I really lost my ship.

Centuries have gone by and the truth has changed many times just like the way he became the captain of *The Black Widow*. Yes, even the truth of Lady Kynan's death. The truth has never been told, but now it is time."

"So you see," Greybellow said, "if the eggs are not placed in their proper places at the proper time, disaster will happen. All of us will be forced to live in the past and the present at the same time for many more years to come. There's not enough time to tell you all the details. You lads and lass need to listen and listen well."

Jerry felt there was something fishy about this so-called test. Zang did not appear to be excited, and the captain had his moments. *Best we have a meeting*, he thought. Quickly, Jerry passed the word to his friends to meet at the edge of the mud pit in ten minutes. Each one made an excuse, and off they went.

Suspecting something was up, Zang and Greybellow climbed a tree to watch the lads and lass to see where they went and what they were doing.

"Do you think we were convincing enough, Greybellow?" Zang questioned.

"Not sure, my friend, not sure."

The first to show up was Jerry. Waiting for the others, he paced and scratched his head, asking himself all kinds of questions.

"What's up?" asked Tom. "Where are the rest?"

"They're coming," Jerry said very impatiently.

Sam and Joey were the next to show up; and finally Cal and Sally arrived.

"Listen," said Jerry, "something is wrong. Something doesn't make a lot of sense. Haven't you noticed how they keep talking about the test without telling us much of anything? They go in circles. Each one tells us his story as if the other one knows nothing . . . like it's top secret stuff. It's nonsense about us being related to the original seven. I don't trust Zang any more than I trust the captain. They are up to no good and treat us like we are their buddies."

"Yeah," said Sally, "and the captain keeps looking at me with funny eyes, and I am not showing him where I hid the eggs either!"

"Zang sticks to us like glue," said Cal.

"I agree," Joey said with a mouth full of Wonder Cakes.

"Anyone have any ideas?" asked Jerry.

"I was hiding in a closet in the captain's quarters," offered Sally, "when I heard the captain talking. He kept saying it wasn't his fault, and if he could change it, he would. I looked through the keyhole and no one was there. The room was filled with trunks. There were books on shelves and all over the floor. Maybe there's something in them that would help us."

"Good idea, Sally," said Jerry. "You and Cal go see what you can find. Go quickly and don't let anyone see you in there!"

"While I was waiting for you guys I explored the galley," Tom told the others. "Did you know there's a secret passage? The walls echo like a mountain valley echoes. That's how I knew you were in trouble. There were also shelves of books with locks on them . . . stuff that smelled weird and looked even weirder.

"I wonder what kind of books needs locks," Jerry questioned.

"There's a bunch of charts and maps. It's the same kind of stuff we found in the caves," yelled Joey.

"You found stuff in the caves?" asked Tom.

"Yeah, when you and Jerry took off, we did our own search. But before we could tell you anything, we all left so I forgot." Joey shrugged his shoulders.

"Great, Joey, now you tell us!" said Sally. "What else did you find in the caves?"

"We didn't go through it all, Sally, because we heard the guys yelling."

"It's too late to go back to the caves," said Jerry. "Maybe there are some clues in the galley too."

"Didn't the captain say that everything had to be put back the way it was before the eggs were stolen or they couldn't go back?" reminded Cal.

"What does that have to do with the caves or the secret passage?" asked Tom.

"I'm not sure," said Sally. "Maybe nothing, but we need to find out and find out in a hurry. We'd better get out of here before Greybellow and Zang come looking for us.

"You're right," warned Sam. "Let's get going!"

CHAPTER 17

"SO FAR, CAPTAIN, they've done well," observed Zang.

"Yes, Zang, and I will be free to be with my beloved and take my place in the English Navy."

"Aye, Captain. And I'll have my ship back! I'll no longer be punished for losing my ship that guarded the magical eggs and feathers or for telling the secrets of the code. The lads and lass still are not sure. Do you think they have time to discover the truth? The feathers—they need to be present for the eggs to work. The magic words are written on them. Do you remember them?" Zang just rambled on and on.

Greybellow quoted: "If the ship goes before the wind, keep her touch tight and her sheets stretched and sail her around Davy Jones Locker, then come about to the stars."

"Yes," said Zang. "When the original pirates read those words, the golden feathers would shine their light, and the golden eggs would give off their magic. I will finally get to show the original pirates that I kept their secrets and told no lies, for the truth will come out and my time spent in the past and present will be over. My spirit will be free to take its place among the stars. The original pirates will measure my life by what I have done, and I will be free."

Sally and Cal returned to the captain's quarters to continue their search. Cal thought of Sally as one of the guys but knew she had the smarts over all of them. She wasn't all that bad to look at either.

"Sally, the new dress you had on the other day, well it really did look pretty on you," Cal said rather shy.

Sally turned and looked at Cal strangely. "No, really, Sally, you were very pretty," said Cal, moving backward out of fear she would produce one of her belches. Blushing, Sally said, "Why, thank you, Cal!"

To Cal's surprise, he swallowed and the lump in his throat disappeared. He smiled once more from ear to ear.

"Let's get to work, Cal."

They dug in cabinet drawers, opened chests, and flipped lids off of crates, but nothing they found seemed important. Frustrated, Sally sat down in the captain's chair, crossed her arms, and put her feet up on the table. Carefully, she leaned back in the chair.

"We're not finding anything to help us, Cal."

"But what are we really looking for, Sally?"

"I don't know. Jerry just said check it out."

"Zang keeps talking about the 'test,' but we haven't been asked to do anything," said Cal.

"Maybe we're not going to be asked to do anything," said Sally. "Maybe we have to find what is missing instead."

"That just doesn't make any sense."

"Wait a minute, Cal!" said Sally. "Sure it does! Just think about it! Each of us found a missing piece of paper with a message, then we found the ship that was missing, next we found the eggs. And remember how the papers connected the eggs. Then we heard Zang talk about the original seven pirates and how we were bound to them. Don't you see? That's it the last piece of the puzzle! We have to find a missing link that connects all this together."

"Now I know why you win all the puzzle contests, Sally."

"Once all these things are linked, Zang can become the captain of *The Black Widow*, if he really is the captain. And Greybellow can go back to the Royal Navy or wherever he goes. But what could it be?"

"Sally, you're so smart, but I just don't understand."

"Hush, Cal, I need to think."

Returning belowdecks, Tom and Sam found themselves in front of the galley door.

"Tom, pull the latch down and the door will open," suggested Sam. Tom touched the latch, and the door swung open. Dust and cobwebs flew out at the boys.

"What are we looking for?" asked Sam.

"Not sure, but whatever it is, it definitely has something to do with the eggs and their magic. They have something to do with Zang and Greybellow leaving this world. Neither one of them is telling us the whole truth."

"How do you figure?"

"It just makes sense, Sam," said Tom. "Look through the books for something stuck between the pages. Try to find unusual words, kinda like the language we found on the pieces of paper. That's how I found the Joshua tree in the cave—I looked for something unusual."

Sam shook his head, but he began pulling books off the shelves, looking through baskets, and shuffling through stack of papers. As he reached for a box high on a shelf, he lost his footing. As he felt himself falling to the floor, he grabbed a ring that hung on the wall. The ring was attached to a chain, which came rolling out of the wall as Sam pulled. To Sam's surprise, the wall started to crackle and move. Tom came running at the sound. Thick dust blew into the air. A door slid open and disappeared into the wall. The boys had dust in their eyes, and the smell of old wood and old papers in their noses. There were cobwebs everywhere.

When the dust settled, Sam was the first to clear his eyes, "Tom, look! It's a secret room!"

They stuck their heads through the doorway, but the experience was like looking into a fishbowl filled with stuff that did not belong there. They looked through walls made of glass, and they could see everything going on in the room. They could see a ship at sea with sailors preparing for sail. Men were climbing the mast unfurling the sails, and a man was on the deck giving orders to other men.

"Look!" cried Sam. "It's Zang! He's at the helm of the ship trying to sail her through a storm. Look at the waves crashing over the deck and the mast! Men are running everywhere. It kinda looks like the ship we're on. This is like looking through a window of time!"

"Look there—up on the mast," shouted Tom. "It's Captain Greybellow! He's tied against the mast with ropes and chains. And the waves are splashing up and over the ship!"

"Tom, look!" urged Sam. "You can see through the deck. Isn't that us down below? We're going to drown! The seawater is coming in through the hatch, but how can that be? We're here! What is Sally doing with those eggs? Are we asleep? Are we dreaming or sleep walking?"

"Do you suppose we are looking at the original pirates?" asked Tom. "This ship has spirit all right! You never know who or what you're going to see next!"

"Beats me, Sam. Let's get out of here. Did you see all those people? They looked like us, but how could that be?"

mumbled Tom. Stepping back slowly and sliding the door shut, both boys stood still in their shoes.

"Did that really happen, Tom?" asked Sam. The dark now became light. "Let me out of here!" he screamed.

***

"Here it is—just what we're looking for, Cal," said Sally. "It's the final piece."

"What's the final piece?" questioned Cal.

"It's a book about pirate souls."

"Let me see!"

Opening the book, Sally turned the pages and began to read. "Zang is the captain of *The Black Widow*, Cal. It says so right here."

"Well, what'sha know about that!"

"Greybellow captured his ship, and guess who he really is? He's a captain in the Royal English Navy."

"What?"

"Yeah, and his ship was called *The Bluebird*. It sunk. The cargo on *The Black Widow* was filled with treasure, and Greybellow was taking it back to England when he was attacked by pirates. There were baskets of breadfruit, pineapples, and pine nuts; barrels of silk thread and fabric on board. And listen to this—there were ostriches onboard . . . special birds that laid golden eggs. A storm came up and carried the ship across the tops of waves onto land, and then over the hollow rocks and through caves and into the mud pit. There is one more thing. This sounds really important, but it is hard to read."

"What is it, Sally?"

"It's something about feathers, I think! I need more light." Cal held the window shutter open and Sally held the book up higher, and she was able to read: "If the ship goes before the wind, keep her touch tight and her sheets stretched and sail her around Davy Jones' Locker, then come about to the stars."

"That's it, Cal!" cried Sally. "That's the answer! Let's get the others."

"Answer to what, Sally?"

"You'll see, Cal . . . you'll see." And Sally flew out the door of the captain's quarters, with Cal following closely behind.

"I thought you said the book was about pirate souls."

"It is! Don't you see? Hurry—let's go."

"It's hot up here on the deck, Jerry! I wonder how pirates stayed cool. Do you think they ate Wonder Cakes or drank cream sodas?"

"Don't be silly, Joey," said Jerry. "They didn't have chocolate or whipped cream back then. Those things weren't invented until sometime after World War I or II—or something like that. I think a man by the name of Hershey thought it up."

"Oh, I bet they did have chocolate cake back in the days of pirates and I bet they had whipped cream too." Joey said with enthusiasm.

"I wonder if any of the others have actually found anything. We're really running out of time, Joey. If you are that hot, why don't you sit under the shade of the sails coming from the main mast. The air will be cooler there."

"Thanks, Jerry!"

Joey was leaning against the canons, eating Wonder Cakes, and dreaming of being a pirate when he saw something. *Umm, something is stuck between the mast and the backside of the bulkhead.* Curious, he crawled on his knees with chocolate smeared on his fingertips and cake stuck between his teeth. Trails of chocolate fingerprints stretched across the deck as he moved closer in on the object. Looking closely between the mast and the bulkhead, Joey saw a book of sorts. Grabbing hold of the edge, he pulled until it popped out of the tight area. He moved back to the cool breeze of the sails and tried to open the book. Turning it over, he realized there was a lock on the front. *Wow—this must be the journal that Sally went up the mast to get from the jaws of the yak.* He went to find Jerry.

"Hey, Jerry, look what I found. It's the journal that Sally pulled from the yak's mouth. When she fell, it fell too and got stuck between the mast and bulkhead. Remember the pieces of paper and what they said? 'Truth lies in the jaws of the yak.' This came from that yak's jaws. Maybe something in here can help."

"Wow, let's see, Joey."

"How are we going to open it? It's locked."

Together, they shook the book, punched it with billy clubs, and poked knives into the lock, but it would not open. Finally they ended up holding onto the book and pulling it back and forth, and arguing about how to get it open. Joey finally jerked the book out of Jerry's hands.

"Let me have it, Jerry! I know how to open it. Just watch!"

Turning toward the main mast, Joey marched over to a large gold ring hanging on the post while Jerry followed close behind.

"There. See? I just remembered," said Joey, pointing to the main mast. There hung a ring of golden keys on a hook. "See? I bet one of those keys matches the lock."

"How did you know about those keys, Joey?"

"I played with them when everyone else was below and I was on watch. When all the commotion started down below, I hung them back on the hook and climbed down the ladder. Then I forgot about them. Look," he said taking down the keys. "See? This key is in the shape of a bird's foot, just like the lock." While Jerry held the book, Joey placed the gold bird-foot key into the lock, turned the key, and—presto—the padlock crackled but did not open.

"Joey, you are awesome," said Jerry. "I can't wait to tell everyone how smart you are and how you figure things out just like Sally!"

Excited now, they sat down and tried the key once more. This time, the lock crackled, snapped, then popped open. Its pages were now free to reveal the truth. Joey began to read.

"Jerry, this is the log book that belongs to the captain of *The Black Widow*. It's the journal of his everyday activities, thoughts, and happenings. Remember the story Zang told us about Greybellow and the capture of Lady Kynan and how she was lost at sea? It's all here in this book. The pieces of paper and the writings we found—see the book's pages are made of the same paper—I think it's called parchment—and the handwriting is the same."

"You know, Joey, I think you're right. Keep reading, buddy."

"The journal says that Zang really is the captain of *The Black Widow*. He won his ship back in a dual with Captain Kilo. When Captain Kilo had *The Black Widow*, there was a battle with an English Royal Navy ship. He stole the cargo and sank the ship. The ship's log shows that Lady Kynan was a passenger onboard that ship. When Zang got the ship back, the crew pledged their loyalties to him, and now they live between the past and present just like him."

"What?" questioned Jerry.

"Yeah, they live forever," said Joey. "Wow listen to this—there was another battle between *The Black Widow* and *The Bluebird*. Guess who was the captain of *The Bluebird*? Captain Greybellow, that's who! It says that Greybellow was in the Royal Navy and served as a captain. He was very powerful and sailed the seas. His sole mission was to destroy all pirates and their ships. He was in search for a captain who had five pirate ships that sailed around the seas of England. He believed it was Zang. The Royal Navy believed it was his ships that were sinking English ships. Greybellow didn't know it was actually Captain Kilo not Zang. During this battle, Kilo took a smaller boat and escaped. Greybellow became a prisoner of *The Black Widow*. This means Greybellow is not a real pirate!"

"It is a good thing you understand, Joey," said Jerry. "I don't understand any of this. I'm very good in finding my way through the forest and figuring out how or what to do in a crisis, but I'm no good at riddles."

"Jerry, it's simple. There were three ships a long time ago, *The Black Widow*, *The Bluebird* and some Royal Navy ship we don't know the name of. *The Black Widow* belonged to

Zang, and he lost it to Captain Kilo in a dual, then he won it back. *The Bluebird* belonged to Captain Greybellow and it was stolen and sunk by Kilo. The unknown ship was part of the Royal Navy. Zang is a pirate, and Greybellow is not," said Joey. "Do you want me to explain everything again?"

"No, but keep on telling me more," requested Jerry.

"Zang betrayed the original pirates. Not much is said how he did. There are hints in the journal that he was one of them, and that he did not keep the pirate secrets, whatever they are. There's a Pirates' Code that says golden eggs and feathers of the golden ostriches are one and connected to a body of honor. 'To yourself be true,' and that is the last line. So when Zang betrayed them, he could not die and join the original pirates. He had to live in the light of the past and present. Greybellow pretended to be a pirate, but gave all the treasure to the poor. He betrayed his own country just like Zang betrayed the Pirates' Code of Honor. If they don't do the right thing by one another now, they will live in the light of the past and present forever. Get it?" explained Joey.

"Really, Joey. That's a lot of stuff! Now it makes sense why they are like they are." Jerry took the log from Joey and examined it.

"Don't you see?" said Joey, "They admired the good in each other. Neither one is as bad as he lets on to be. Because of the date, this will be their last chance for a very long time."

"Boy, it is a good thing you read a lot of mystery books," said Jerry. "I would never have figured that one out. You're okay, Joey, you're okay," Jerry said with enthusiasm. Let me read some and see what I can find."

"Fine, I get it . . . tired of listening to me?" Joey spouted off.

"Hey, look at this, Joey, it says the golden eggs have powers. There's a different power for each egg. There's something about feathers of an ostrich, but it is hard to read. Didn't you already read this earlier? Must be something else we missed. Can you read this?"

"Let me see!" Joey grabbed the book and began to read. "Oh, my gosh! This is how it's done!"

"How what's done?"

"We need to get the others here now. It'll take all of us, and what we all know."

"Know what Joey?" asked Jerry as they started to run after the others.

"Come on," yelled Joey. "I'll tell you as we run back."

CHAPTER 18

G RABBING JERRY'S ARM, Joey took off running
toward the meeting place. Sally and Cal jumped off
the ship shouldering a large book between them and went
running. At the heels of Cal were Tom and Sam running
and waving their arms and screaming something no one
could understand. When they met up, everyone began
talking at once trying to tell what they learned. No one
was listening.

Jerry finally yelled, "*Shut up!* This is not getting us
anywhere. Stop talking and listen, okay? Sally, you go first.
What did you and Cal find?"

"Cal and I searched the captain's quarters, but we really
couldn't find anything so we sat down at the table to figure
it out. There were lots of bowls, books, and cups thrown all
over the table, and there it was right in front of our eyes."

"What are you talking about, Sally?" question Sam.

"Under a stack of books I saw something that looked
different. Remember that Jerry told us to look for something
that doesn't belong? The thing that caught my eye was
the cover. It was made of feathers. How weird is that? As I
looked closer, I realized the feathers were actually stuck to
a leather book. I opened the book and the paper was gold

parchment just like the stuff that our messages were written on. Several pages had been torn, and I began to read the pages. The words in the book were the same as the words in our messages. I flipped through the book, and near the back there were pages torn out. I recognized the torn edges. I took my message from my pocket and put it against one of the torn edges, and guess what happen? The paper fit the torn page. That's when I realized all our messages came from this book. The book tells how people become pirates, how they live as pirates, and how they must die as pirates. There are pirate codes, their secrets—and listen to this! When they die, the golden eggs keep their souls, and their spirits go to a star with seven points. The star guides all sailors that follow the Pirates' Code. Then there was something about ostrich feathers too."

"Sally is onto something," said Tom "When Sam and I were in the galley, a weird thing happened that you've just got to see! You won't believe it! There is a secret chamber onboard. It's hidden behind a door in the narrow hallway that leads into the galley. The door slides between the walls."

Then Sam jumped in and described what he had seen. "We could see our past and our present. We could see Greybellow tied to the mast. The weird thing was that there were people who looked just like us in the cargo hull doing all kinds of stuff. Sally, you had something in your hands and you were brushing eggs. Jerry, you were drawing a star, and Joey . . . well you were reading from a book. Everyone there in that secret chamber looked just like us. I tell ya, the chamber has something to do with what is happening to us. I'm telling you, it was weird to see our own look-alikes. Maybe the feathers, the eggs, and all of us are connected to the forefathers in the chamber."

"I think we are," said Joey. "You will not believe what we found on deck!" Joey pulled a brown, leather-bound book from behind his back.

"What is it?" asked Tom.

"It's the ship's journal written by Zang," said Joey.

"How do you know Zang wrote it?" asked Tom.

"Because he was the true captain of *The Black Widow* just like it said in the book Sally read. See the padlock? It's in the shape of an ostrich foot, and the key on this ring matches the lock. It was meant for us to find the journal as well as Sally's book."

"Things are adding up," said Jerry. "Okay, it looks like that each of us found something that is tied into the others. There is the Pirates' Code Book, the journal, and a chamber filled with mysteries. How much time do we have left? Anyone know?"

"Time is moving fast, and I think we are down to hours," stated Joey.

"Let's go to the chamber and see if Sally can put the puzzle together," said Sam.

"What do you think, Sally, can you do it?" asked Sam.

"You bet!" she said. "But I feel that Zang and Greybellow are around. I feel it in my bones, and I'm still not sure if they are with us or against us. Let's go, and I'll do my best, Joey. Will you help?" asked Sally.

"You bet, little Sis."

"I remember reading in the journal that all things must be in place by the seventh day of the seventh month," explained Cal. "Isn't that today? If it is, we have only about two hours or so."

"Let's get cracking," said Jerry. "There's not much time left. Besides it's my birthday! And what a birthday it'll be!"

Climbing back onto the ship, everyone was pushing and shoving, when they suddenly found Zang and Greybellow standing smack in front of their path glaring each of them down.

"What's up?" questioned Jerry.

"Where are going?" Greybellow inquired.

"Uh, nowhere, sir," said Joey. "We're just fooling around. Today is Jerry's birthday. Can you beat that?"

"I see ya found my ship's log, matey," said Zang pointing to the book Joey held almost all the way behind his back.

"Captain, looky thar, the little lass is holding the Pirates' Code Book!"

"You can't have it," screamed Sally, holding the book out to Zang. "And I know that you are not a pirate, Captain. I know who you are!"

Eyebrows raised, shoulders back, and standing tall, Greybellow glared at Sally. "Do ya, lass!" he said. Then he looked back at Zang. "Looks like we have snoopers onboard."

"Hand me my log, matey," blurted Zang, holding his hand out to Joey.

"No way!" screamed Jerry. "Not until we finish. Don't give it to him, Joey."

Greybellow placed his arm across Zang's chest. "Wait—he's right. If they don't finish, we won't go back. Then he turned to the lads and lass. "The feathers," he said. "Did ya find 'em?"

"No, that's why we're going to the chamber," said Jerry.

"Chamber, what chamber?" asked the captain.

Sam blurted out what they had found in the galley, "It's a secret chamber and it shows the past as well as the present."

"You mean to say it shows the past *and* the present?" said Greybellow as he laughed out loud. "Now, that would be something to see. I suppose the Royal Navy and all her ships are in this chamber too."

"Yes, that's right," Sam replied in a soft voice. "Maybe you could learn the whereabouts of Lady Kynan."

"We even saw you, Captain Greybellow," said Tom. "You were in the chamber, and you were tied to the mast. You should come with us."

"Zang," roared Greybellow, "if that chamber shows that ya killed her, you'll not find your spirit in the stars—but in hell!"

Looking back at the captain, Zang replied, "I have told you for centuries that I did not kill her."

"We shall see," said Greybellow, "we shall see!"

And he turned again to the kids. "Since you found this chamber and have the idea that it is connected to the Pirates' Code Book and the journal, then lead the way." Greybellow bowed from his waist as he said, "I want to see this chamber."

"Time is running out," warned Zang. "We should hurry."

"This way," Jerry said, and off they all went.

CHAPTER 19

TOM AND SAM led the way: down the stairs, past the bulkhead, into the galley, and finally into the narrow hallway. Old books, papers, and barrels were strewn everywhere. Someone kicked a barrel, and dust was stirred with thick cobwebs.

"The air is still so thick and heavy," said Sam. Coughing and holding his hands over his nose and mouth, Sam kept moving using his arms and hands to clear the way. Cal rubbed the dust from his eyes as he tried to keep an eye on Sally, who was holding the ship's journal under one arm and the Pirates' Code Book under the other. It was obvious that he was afraid that Zang would try to grab the books away from Sally. Knowing the importance of the books, Sally and Jerry had agreed that he should keep the key to the journal for safety. He had attached it to his belt. Greybellow and Zang followed close by watching all their moves.

The hallway narrowed and became dark. Feeling for the oil lamp that he remembered being on the wall, Tom found a small candle and lit it with the match from a holder. Sam felt along the other wall trying to find the oil lamp. "Here it is!" he said. "Give me a match, Tom, or the candle." Sam turned the small wheel on the oil lamp. The wick moved upward, and he lit the wick with Tom's candle. He noticed there was still oil in the bowl of the lamp. Sam walked slowly down the hallway with his candle.

"Even with this light, I can't seem to find the ring," said Sam. In a few minutes he found it. Everyone gathered close by. Greybellow and Zang seemed as anxious as the kids.

"Stop!" yelled Sally. "What if this is a mistake?"

"We have no choice," said Jerry. "It's either finish this thing once and for all, or give up. If we give up, Zang and Greybellow are stuck. And who knows? We may be stuck with them. We've come this far. Why not show 'em what we're made of?"

Sam pulled on the ring, but nothing happened.

"Try again, Sam!" urged Tom. This time, when Sam pulled down on the ring, the walls crackled, and the door started to slide. It moved inside the wall and disappeared. Everyone's eyes opened wide, and mouths dropped. One by one, they climbed over one other trying to peek through the door only to find nothing was there.

"What?" said Cal. "Where's the past? There's nothing! What's going on?"

"Move over and let me see," said Tom.

"Wait, me too. I want to see," spouted Sally.

"What do you think happened, Sam?" asked Tom.

Sam scratched his head. "Beat's me."

"Are you sure we're in the right place? This looks more like the storage hull filled with food and supplies. There is nothing in here but rye and flour sacks and barrels," said Greybellow.

"This is strange," said Sam as he scratched his head.

"Are you sure you two weren't dreaming?" Joey asked as he stuffed his hands into his pockets and leaned against the wall. At the same time, he lost his footing and started falling backward. He reached out for anything that would stop his fall, and grabbed the edge of the sliding door.

"Look!" yelled Sally. "The sliding door didn't slide all the way; it got stuck!" Joey pushed and tugged until it was free and slid it into the wall. With a loud click and some bright lights, little by little, everything changed. The chamber of the past and present appeared, and there it was—the ship—just as Tom and Sam had said.

"See? We weren't lying," boasted Tom. "There it is, just as big as you please."

"As long as I have been on this ship, I've never seen this!" cried out Zang in disbelief.

"Look, Zang, you're at the helm!" yelled Sam.

Everyone watched Zang as he steered *The Black Widow* into the wind. The crew released the large sails toward the horizon and set the ship in motion. In the light of the sunrays was another ship.

"Whose ship is that?" Zang asked. "But it looks like—"

Tom interrupted. "There, see? Cal and Sally are in the hull of the ship."

Sam looked around for the whereabouts of Greybellow. "Look at the main mast, Greybellow. It's you!" said Sam.

"What'sha make of this Greybellow?" asked Zang.

"Ah . . . not sure," came the reply

"Can we touch anything?" Sally reached out into the air.

"Careful, Sally," said Tom.

"Wow, look! It's me carrying the eggs," said Sally.

"Listen, you can hear what is being said," whispered Jerry. "Quiet . . . listen!"

"Keep the loot below, mateys," yelled Zang in the chamber.

"Sam, you are carrying a golden box in your arms," said Tom. An eerie feeling came over Sam as he looked at his own reflection.

"Tom, do you remember all the pictures of our family that Mom hung on the staircase at home?" asked Cal.

"Yeah, but is this really the time to bring up pictures of our family?" asked Tom.

"Just listen. Remember when Mom did the ancestry study and found pictures of our relatives? She believed one of them was our great-something-or-other-grandfather, Sandy.

Well, doesn't the guy with the ropes in his hands look like that picture of Sandy?"

"Yeah, it does look like him from what I can remember."

Jumping into the conversation, Sam pointed at a guy sitting on a barrel. A set of crossbones dangled from a chain around his neck. "He looks a lot like my great-great-grandfather Murdie. I've got a picture of him on my nightstand."

"The tall, lanky guy with the black vest and a sword hanging from a red sash on his hip—he looks like me!" said Jerry as he pinched himself to see if he was here or there. "It is weird how we all kinda look like them. That has to be my Dad's great-great-grandpop, Maurice. We sometimes called him Decess."

Joey was pulling a Wonder Cake out to settle his nerves when, over in the corner, he noticed a rather jolly old guy eating a cake that chocolate smears all over his mouth. Hey, Poppy!" yelled Joey. The old man looked up and smiled, then tipped his hat. "I feel like I'm looking in the mirror!" said Joey. Smiles of chocolate cake showed on both of their faces.

"I don't see anyone who looks like me!" Sally said sadly. "Wait! Who is that bending over the eggs brushing them off? Hey, guys, look! That's a woman, and it has to be Mama Ela; I think she is my great-great-grandmother!" Turning and smiling at Sally, Mama Ela pointed to the eggs and motioned for her to come nearer. It was hard to tell if what they were looking at was real or not. "Everyone looks so much like us," said Sally. "But how could that be? They are from another time and so long ago. We must really have some good genes in our bloodlines—or is it like Zang said . . . sometimes we see what we want to see?"

Cal was holding the door taking all this in when it hit him. "I agree with Sally. It isn't a test, but how we relate to one another that forms the magic—the eggs, the feathers, and us, that's what makes the magic work. Isn't that right, Sally?" asked Cal.

"You know, Cal . . ." Sally paused. "You're right! Don't you see? In the books, over and over they talked about pirates' honor, trust, leadership, and loyalty. All those things may be in the messages, but that is who we are!" explained Sally. "And that is why we see what we are seeing—*ourselves* in the past. You see, both Greybellow and Zang are tied together, and they don't even know it! Both shattered the Pirates' Code of trust, honor and loyalty by pretending to be something they are not."

"What are you talking about, Sally?" asked Joey.

"In order for Zang and Greybellow to return," explained Sally. "Zang had to find us. We live by the Pirates' Code and prove that every day it's part of us. That could only be because we are from the lineage of the original pirates. Our forefathers put their secrets of the sea, their souls, their hearts, and their honor under the protection of the golden eggs and the feathers," explained Sally. "It was their treasure to be given only to those who were deserving. Zang and Greybellow were to keep them safe until we were found. Only then can they return to their proper place in time."

"Oh, but aren't we missing some eggs?" asked Cal.

Sally stared at everyone. "It won't work if we don't have all the eggs as well as the feathers with us at the same time. This is what they want us to see—that by looking at our past we can fix the present. You see, the golden eggs and feathers are working their magic now. *This* is the magic. They can control our present by changing the past. That is why we are here."

"If you ask me, that's pretty deep, Sally," said Joey.

Looking straight at Zang, Greybellow asked, "Zang, what about it? Are you ready to tell the truth and give the eggs up so you can join the original pirates? Or are you going to stay here for another who-knows-how-many years swearing that I have the eggs?"

"Wow, Sally, you are a real pro at this," said Cal.

"Everything you are saying may be true," said Zang, "But I don't have the eggs! I have been trying to find them for more than two centuries by following you—only to come up short . . . no eggs and no feathers.

"That's where you made the first mistake, Zang," Greybellow answered back. "You never fooled me or the original pirates!"

"Greybellow," countered Zang. "You're not a pirate, and everyone knows it. It's time for you and me to put things right. We've been here long enough. Where are the eggs?" I know you have 'em hidden somewhere!"

Greybellow looked away from Zang, annoyed at his suggestion that he had been lying. "Lass, where did ya get these ideas?" asked Greybellow.

"Just look around us, Captain Greybellow," said Sally. This room is not real. It is what our forefathers want us to see. They are trying to help us get you back to your ship and to Lady Kynan. It is time for Zang to join them in the heaven of stars."

"I think I get it," said Cal. "Look, Captain Greybellow, our ancestors started the Pirates' Code of Honor. When Zang lost his ship, *The Black Widow*, and betrayed that code of honor and trust, he lost face, and lost the respect of all the other pirates. You did the same thing by betraying your country and not doing what was right by your king. And when that happened . . . well it all got broken. The bond you and Zang share is what got you in this mess. Don't you understand the importance of all this? Surely you aren't that blind. Everything must be put back in the right place, and the truth must be told before you can return."

"You know about the golden eggs, the feathers, and who we really are," added Jerry.

Zang turned and looked at Greybellow. "It's time, and you know it," he said. "There is no more testing, and the chamber confirmed who these lads and lass are. You have known all along?"

Greybellow grabbed Zang's shirt. "Guess your right Zang. You'd better be. Come with me." He turned to the lads and lass. "You stay here. We'll be back." Zang hung his head very low as Greybellow spoke. The kids could tell Zang must feel shame, for he did not know how to respond to Greybellow.

Just as the two of them started to leave the chamber, the ship started to rock forward and the door to the hallway and cargo hull started to shut.

"Quick!" yelled Zang. "Someone grab the door before the ship moves again, or we'll never get out! As they all stretched their arms in search of something to grab onto, the ship rolled again backward and forward as it rode the waves of the sea heading for the mud pit.

"Hold on! She's moving with greater force! My spell is breaking up!" yelled Zang. "Grab the ladder!" As the ship pitched down, mud and water came splashing onto the decks. Everyone below was tossed in different directions.

Tumbling into the cargo boxes, nets, and barrels of liquid, Greybellow yelled, "Hold on f'r your life! The ship is coming about!" They all grabbed posts, rope netting, barrels . . . anything they could. And the tumbling continued.

Falling to the floor, Sally screamed loud, "This isn't fun anymore! I want to go home!"

"Me too," said Joey, upchucking his last Wonder Cake.

"The ship is moving back into the mist of the mud pit!" yelled Jerry as he reached out and caught the corner of the door just before it tried to shut. "Caught it!" he yelled.

Jamming his foot between the door and the wall, he managed to pull his way through the doorway before the door slammed shut. Jerry could hear everyone tumbling and screaming on the other side of the door. He tried to reopen the door, but it wouldn't budge. He knew the only chance to free everyone was to climb up to the deck and open the cargo hull hatch. The ship rolled again port to starboard. Over and over, the ship rocked and rolled. Jerry knew his friends were in trouble, and he was their only chance.

Tom looked up and saw a light coming through the cargo hull hatch. It was opening!

"Hello down below," yelled Jerry. "You guys okay?" The sun was bright, and no one could see who it was.

"Jerry, how did you get up there?" asked Cal, when he finally recognized his friend.

"Tell ya later, Cal. Let's get you guys out of there before it's too late. Look out down below here comes the ladder." Climbing over each other and scrambling over the cargo boxes, they made their way to the ladder.

"Is everyone okay and intact?" asked Jerry.

"Hold on! Here we go again!" said Tom.

The ship rocked one more time, then settled down into the mud. Joey was crying, and Sally was holding onto Cal as tightly as she could. They all stood there in despair, not knowing what was next.

"Where did everyone go?" asked Tom. The magic of our past, what happen to it?

Zang spoke up from behind the children. "When the ship started to move, the spell of the ship was broken, and everything went back to where it belonged—to the past," he said. He stood up, grabbed Greybellow by the shoulder, and told the kids to stay on shore where the ship was last seen and stay there.

"We're gonna get the eggs and the feathers!" Zang yelled. "We know what we must do now. Ya just stay there. Ye'll be all right. Just stay put. You have everything ya need, and we'll hurry."

CHAPTER 20

AS THE SHIP settled down, so did the nerves of the kids. They did as they were told—climbed onto shore and "stayed put," as Zang had said. They even began to smile as the sun began to shine. It was difficult to see at first, but before them, there they stood the original pirates.

"How did they get here?" asked Cal. "I thought the spell was broken."

"Through the light, Cal!" said Sally. "Still don't get it, do you Cal? This isn't sunlight! It's the radiant light that is produced by the golden eggs. It's that light that allows us to see the original pirates."

The pirates stood in the light, each in his place on the deck of *The Black Widow*. It had been their ship, and Zang had been the captain. The great ship had kept them safe for centuries. It was time for the process to start. Through the bright light, a stronger beam of light struck the deck. At the end of the beam, a formation began to take shape . . . it was the seven-point star. At the top of the star stood Pop Maurice and Jerry. To their right stood Grandpa Sandy with Tom and his brother Cal. Poppy was with Joey, and Granddad Murdie was with Sam. In the middle, Mama Ela stood with Sally.

"There are only five points of the star shining," said Sally. "Who lights up the other two points?"

"Sally, remember Thomas the pirate who died by the hand of the king?" asked Cal. "He is there in the star. Look closer and you can see, Sally."

"If that is so, who lights up the last point?" Sally spoke very sternly. "And where have Zang and Greybellow gone?"

Zang sat near the edge of the embankment where the weeping willows parted with their branches bowing over the green beds of gooey slime. As he watched Greybellow throw rocks into the water, his thoughts wandered. *Can I trust Greybellow?* he asked himself. *The lads and lass have done their jobs, as I knew they would. Using their heads, hearts, and minds, they showed that they carried all the trademarks and secrets of the original pirates, and this information has been passed down from generation to generation as promised.* Zang had seen many men come and go, but not until these lads and lass showed up did he realize he'd finally found the right souls. *But can they really set us free? There isn't time to argue with Greybellow. I'll just have to trust him.*

Greybellow had one foot in the green, gooey slime and the other in clear water as he picked up boulders and rocks and threw them in the water.

"You could help me," stated Greybellow, struggling to breathe. "Since we both know it's you who has the eggs and not I!"

"If you think that, Greybellow, why are you throwing all those rocks? Besides, maybe I do and maybe I don't have 'em," said Zang.

"Look, Zang," said Greybellow, "we have no time left—as you so well pointed out—to play games. I *do* have the golden feathers, but I don't have the eggs, and they are hidden here. I saw you hide the eggs in the water trees. That's when I decided that the best place to hide the feathers was right near the eggs. No one would ever think to look in the same place for both. So get off your butt and get the eggs! I'm ready to be with my beloved."

"Stop throwing rocks into the water," said Zang. "They aren't there. How did you know that the eggs can't work without the feathers?" he asked.

"It was your journal," admitted Greybellow. "I read how you betrayed the original pirates and they placed you in limbo as punishment. But I was not ready to reveal that I knew because I had to know who really killed Lady Kynan and stole the treasure out from under me."

"So you think you know?" wondered Zang out loud. Zang shook his head and smiled that crooked smile as he moved into the water toward the water trees.

There were five trees with large trunks and roots folding over one another making large loops and knots. Lighting had long ago hit one of the bigger trees and split the trunk into the shape of a fork. Over time, the openings had grown larger and deeper. Each crevice had filled with moss, grass, and twigs that were blown by the wind. Sea foam had pushed its way deep into the crevices. This had protected the eggs from man and weather over time. It was here that Zang had placed the rest of the golden eggs. He had put the counterfeit eggs in the swamp and in the caves to make sure no one knew the real secret hiding place. He had given the other eggs the power of light to fend off the thieves and throw them off the track of the real eggs. Crawling over the large roots, Zang made his way to the forked tree. Brushing moss away, pulling debris out, and digging deep under the sea foam and into the hole, he reached for the leather crate filled with eggs. "There it is I can feel it!" he said.

But the stench of mud and slime was more than he could bear. Pulling away and wrapping his shirt around his head to cover his nose and mouth, Zang stuck his hands and arms back down into the hole and gently pulled the leather crate up and out to the surface. Lugging the heavy burden, he climbed down from the water tree and waded out of the water. He laid the leather crate on the ground. After using his shirttail to clean his hands, one by one, he removed the eggs from the crate to ensure they were safe. And safe they were. None had been broken or damaged from the years being in the hole or from the storms that had washed the debris over them. *I can breathe with relief,* thought Zang. *It has been a long time since I have laid my eyes upon them!* "Here are the eggs," said Zang. "Now get the golden feathers!"

Greybellow looked at Zang with content as he started his climb into the willow trees. The trees were thick with long limbs that hung over the top of the water trees creating a canopy. Some of the limbs had rooted and become new trees with fresh green limbs. Eagles loved the willow trees, and would build their nests in the tops of the trees. In fact, there was a nest of young chicks at the top of one of the trees. The larger nest was the oldest; it had seen its days of young eagles come and go. The limbs were still strong, and the tree was the perfect place to hide the feathers. Just under the nest to the right of the largest limb was a flour sack bound entirely in leather straps to protect the sack from coming apart over time. It had been pushed deep between the limbs for safety and tied in place. It looked just like the other limbs of the willow tree. With the old eagle nest empty, Greybellow was able to position himself in the tree to dig deep between the limbs for the golden feathers. He began to untangle the knots to loosen the ropes that secured the sack. Very carefully he pulled the sack out from the limbs and placed it on top of the eagles' nest. "Zang, come help with the sack," he yelled down. "My feet are stuck in the green slime and tangled in the branches."

"You put 'em there, you bring 'em down," snickered Zang.

Reaching carefully, Greybellow managed to pull the sack from the eagles' nest, open it, and secure the feathers inside his shirt. Then he started climbing down the tree. He had read and heard stories about the magic of the eggs and feathers for centuries, but he never knew whether or not they were real. This would be the first time he would see the eggs and feathers together. "Can they really control our past as well as our present?" he wondered aloud.

Down on the ground and safe, Greybellow opened his shirt. The magic light shone brightly as he pulled the seven feathers out one by one and laid them side by side on the ground. Zang carefully removed the eggs one at a time from the leather crate and placed each one of them onto one the feathers. Watching the magic of the golden eggs and feathers unite gave Zang and Greybellow a strange feeling. All the bitterness between them began to fade.

"There must be some truth about these eggs and feathers, Zang," admitted Greybellow. "I feel alive for the first time in centuries. And I'm experiencing strange feelings of peace."

"You know, you really weren't a bad pirate," said Zang. "You gave much of what you took to those in need, but you just did not know the real truth about me, *The Black Widow*, or Lady Kynan. Not knowing the truth is what always got in your way. Maybe now it is time you knew." Settling down on a rock, and indicating with his hand for Greybellow to join him, Zang decided to tell the truth about Lady Kynan.

Zang began his story: "Captain Kilo had stolen my ship in a wild card game. Using my ship, Kilo showed his true colors as a thief when he stole gold from the king and jewels from his treasury. He wanted power! Kilo was a jealous man, and his hatred for the English and you is what drove him. He swore to sink English ships and to kill the English sailors when he found them. He did not stop there. He killed for pleasure, including anyone who got in his way. He was a mean one, he was. He had no regard for the Pirates' Code of Honor.

He came upon Lady Kynan's ship and boarded her with the intent of looting, taking the women to sell as slaves, killing darn good sailors, and torturing the captain. Later I met up with Kilo and got my ship back in a dual to the death. When he showed up for the dual, he refused to play by the rules. He threw his sword as if it was a dagger and tried to hit my heart! Missed it, he did, and disappeared. I never saw him again!

When you found Lady Kynan's ship and swore revenge, you were not ready to hear the truth because your heart had turned black with pain. So I waited. It was my ship but I was not there. I saw you board her from another and the rest you know." Tears in his eyes, Greybellow listened and said nothing. Finally, turning to Zang, he said, "We'd better go. Its time." and no more was said.

Returning to *The Black Widow*, Greybellow carried the golden ostrich feathers near his heart, causing a bright light to radiate through his shirt. Zang carried the precious golden eggs in the leather crate. From a distance, Zang could see that the transformation of the Pirates' Star had begun. Everyone had taken his place … Sally and Mama Ela were standing at the empty crates waiting for the golden eggs to be returned to their rightful places.

"Quick, Greybellow, we must hurry," urged Zang. "It has started!" As they ran and helped each other over logs, across holes, and through slippery slime, their friendship began to reappear. The truth had been set free, and their hearts had begun to heal.

When Greybellow and Zang finally arrived on the deck of *The Black Widow* with the golden ostrich feathers and the golden eggs, Sally motioned to the men to lay them on the crate where the golden parchments lay.

"Everyone stand at your place and let the words of the Pirates' Code of Honor begin," instructed Sally as she smiled at Mama Ela.

Greybellow and Zang took their places. Jerry took charge as he always did, and read the first verse of the Pirates' Code. Motioning to Joey, he read about the importance of being together, sharing lives. He read how this sort of bond would give them power. Cal then spoke of the leadership and brotherhood that had been passed down from the original pirates. He reminded everyone that the spirit of these traits from the original pirates was still strong, alive, and well. Tom, standing next to Sandy, spoke of the importance of thinking things through to solve differences. He spoke about the importance of using common sense. Sam took a stride toward Murdie as he spoke of the importance of believing in yourself, being truthful, and most of all being true to yourself. Finally, Sally held the glue that kept them together. With a warm heart, gentle mind, and with determination, their friendship would last a lifetime, and this was the gift from Mama Ela. The words of the Pirates' Code grew stronger as they were spoken by the lads and lass who were blood descendants of the original pirates. The original pirates could feel the courage, trust, and loyalty that each one possessed. These traits still lived on through their kinsman. All those present were in their places. As Sally recited the final passages, a voice shouted, "It's Captain Kilo!"

Zang turned and yelled, "Kilo! It was you I smelled on *The Black Widow*! This is one time you aren't taking my ship. I knew you weren't dead all these years. I could smell ya!"

"Aye, it's me," said Kilo as he drew his sword, "and I intend to stay here! And that means you and these mateys and that lass must die!" With that said, Kilo lunged toward the kids with his sword in hand. "You first," he shouted. "The one who thinks he knows the forest! I'll skewer you through the heart like an animal!"

Quickly, Jerry ducked and fell to his back, tripping Kilo with his feet. Kilo hit the deck with a loud thump, but was up again, wiping his face with his sleeve. Then he reached out and grabbed Sally around the waist. "It will be her or you, laddie," he said to Jerry. "Makes no difference to me." Jerry sprang to his feet and dove straight for Kilo.

"Ya won't hurt a hair on their heads!" shouted Zang as he swung his sword in an attempt to drive Kilo back. He lunged forward, but Kilo struck back, cutting Zang on the arm.

"Don't you hurt him!" Sally bit down hard on Kilo's arm.

"Blast ya, girlee!" Kilo picked up his sword and struck a blow at Sally. Zang pulled her to the ground just as the sword flew over her head.

"No!" screamed Greybellow, drawing his sword. "You will not hurt her or any of these lads, Kilo. If it's a fight you want, I'll give you one." Lunging forward, Greybellow waved his sword in circles at Kilo. Their swords clanking, their feet moving from side to side with the quickness of the wind, with twists and turns, the fight was a vigorous battle. Kilo jumped up onto a barrel, but Greybellow suddenly came forward and struck him through the heart. Kilo fell to the ground, and his body burned to dust.

Zang looked at Greybellow with that crooked smile and he was heard to say, "Greybellow, I knew you were a good guy and would only fight for the right. You are truly my friend. You defended me and the lads and lass to the end as a brave Royal Navy captain."

The original pirates stepped forward, "You have proven your loyalty as well as your trust for others," said Sandy. "You have replaced your pain with honor."

Then Maurice spoke. "For your bravery and for showing how truth overcomes all, we wish to bestow on you the rank of commodore."

Thomas moved out of the light. "For we are subjects of the king and hold rank in his court, and now it is time for you to return and take your place in the kings' English Royal Navy," he said.

Before everyone's eyes, Greybellow started to change. He no longer stood wearing pirate gear. His clothes transformed into an English Royal Navy commodore's uniform consisting of a deep-blue coat with white and red velvet lapels, gold braid, and brass buttons. His shirt was of white ruffled silk, and his trousers were made of black, shiny material. Gold metals hung from his lapels. A large black hat with white plumes of ostrich feathers sat upon his head. His boots came to his knees and shined so brightly you could see your face in them. He truly was a Royal Navy commodore and a beautiful site to see.

"The magic of the eggs and feathers really works!" Sally cried out.

There was a glow about Greybellow. As everyone stood there looking at him, they heard a voice. "Thaddeus, my love." When they turned, they saw Lady Kynan standing in the bright light. She was wearing a beautiful emerald-green dress. Pearls as white as snow strung on golden rib-bone string hung from her neck. Her hair was golden-red and fell loosely over her shoulders and down her back. A soft smile dominated her face as she looked at Commodore Greybellow.

Jerry whispered to Sally, "She looks like you."

Sally whispered back, "With that golden-red hair, I see where he thought I looked like her."

Looking deep into Greybellow's eyes and into his heart, Lady Kynan held out her arms for him to come to her. "You came for me with honor in your heart," she said. "The pain is gone, and the love has returned. You saved the master of the forest as well as Sally, the great-great granddaughter of Mama Ela." Kynan spoke with a gentle voice of honor. "Come take your place next to me!"

"Aye, I agree it is time," said Sandy. "You, Commodore Greybellow, and Zang have mended the Pirates' Code of Honor. You have become true to yourselves."

"The truth you now know," said Maurice. "Zang did not kill Lady Kynan. But he did step forward to defend his honor as well as the children of our blood. Kilo took your ship, Greybellow, and put Kynan in our light."

"The loyalty and friendship you have shown to Zang, our seventh original pirate," explained Mama Ela, "will be eternal. Go in the light with your love and find peace. The return of the golden eggs and golden feathers has earned you this power."

The original pirates took the hands of their kinsman and formed the Pirate Star as they recited the pledges of the Pirates' Code. As they spoke, the transformation began. With Commodore Greybellow in the center, arm in arm with Lady Kynan, the magic of the golden eggs and feathers began. The two were lifted into the bright and changing light high above the clouds never to be seen again.

"The past was corrected by the present, just like the book said it would," said Sally.

"It is done," said Zang." The original pirates kept their promise and worked the magic with the golden eggs and feathers." Everyone watched Greybellow and Lady Kynan disappear into the light to join all the other pirate souls that had been trapped between the past and the present with him. All it had taken was truth, honor, and loyalty for the commodore to return and the pirate souls to move into the star. Zang stood proudly with his hat across his chest and his skull and crossbones medallion in hand. "God Bless ya, Greybellow."

CHAPTER 21

T HE ORIGINAL PIRATES looked at Zang with compassion. "Now for you," said Sandy.

"Where are the missing pages of the pirate code book?" asked Maurice. "We know you took them centuries ago!"

"Aye, I did take 'em," admitted Zang. "I thought you had turned your backs on me when my ship was taken with all its treasure. It was wrong of me. I should've taken my punishment for telling Kilo the secret passageways of the seas and the ways of pirates' travel. If I hadn't told, I would never be in this mess." Zang spoke with sadness in his voice. "I hid the missing pages between the golden parchment that the eggs sat on for safekeeping. Here, I'll show you." One by one, he peeled back the edges and the missing pages were revealed with the magic words. The light of the pirate book pulled each page back to its proper place. Now the book that was the Pirates' Code of Honor was once more.

"Zang, Captain Kilo's heart was a bad heart," explained Murdie. "For a true thief he was, and for that reason the pirate codes and the magic words did not work for him.

"You see," Mama Ela began to speak, "you only betrayed yourself. That betrayal has kept you between the past and present for centuries. You found your way back by telling

Commodore Greybellow the truth about *The Black Widow* and Lady Kynan, and by finding our true bloodlines to prove that the Pirates' Code is still strong and well. It was the truth that kept you from us, and it was the truth that set you free. You have redeemed your soul by allowing trust, honor, loyalty, and a warm heart back in your spirit. We are ready for you to join us."

"Zang," questioned Sally, "did that really happen?"

"Yes, my dearie. The powers are strong, and the pirate ethics are even stronger," he said with pride.

"But why haven't you gone?" asked Jerry.

"Don't be sad, Zang," said Joey. "Want a Wonder Cake?"

Turning to the kids and looking each one of them in the eye, Zang told them what he had done years and years ago.

"What a shame," Sally said softly.

"Time is something you cannot measure," explained Zang. "But it is all round us, and what you do with that time matters. Where there is truth, it will come out no matter how you measure it. Always remember, Sally, sometimes what you think you see or believe isn't real at all!"

"That makes no sense!" said Sally. "Just how do you propose to go back? Look around you. Where are the original pirates? And where is *The Black Widow* now? I can see clearly it isn't here."

"Don't ya worry your pretty little head, dearie," said Zang. "I have it all in my pocket." He padded the oversized pockets of his coat. His smile was crocked as usual, but his expression was also filled with curiosity. "You see, dearie, the original pirates know that there are more eggs and feathers that are magic. They are part of me just like the book of the Pirates' Code. The original pirates made me Guardian of the golden eggs and golden ostrich feathers. I am the protector of things then and now—of thoughts and souls of pirates from the beginning of time. It is the power given to me by the original pirates."

"Wow!" said Jerry. "So, what now?"

"We need to get back to the ship before it's too late," Zang said.

"Hasn't the ship gone back to the mud pit with all the pirates?" asked Cal.

"Weren't we on *The Black Widow* when Commodore Greybellow left?" asked Tom.

"You ask too many questions," said Zang. "Remember what I said, lads and lass. What you think you see with your eyes is not always real. But it is time for you to see how the magic really works."

Zang took the eggs and feathers from his pockets and laid them on the ground very carefully. He placed the feathers across each other forming the pirate cross and then he centered the eggs in a V shape with the smallest part of the eggs touching in the center. Then he pulled the Pirates' Code Book from his pocket;

"Hey, how did you get that?" asked Joey. "Give it back!"

"Just wait, Joey, and watch," said Zang; then he started to recite: "The clouds darken turning dark gray and formed heavy fog over the horizon. The foggy mist rolled over the marsh and into the mud pit once more."

"Look!" yelled Sam. "Over there in the corner of the mud pit! It's *The Black Widow*!"

"Let's go, kids," said Zang quickly.

"How did he do that?" Cal asked Tom.

"Look around you," said Zang. There stood all the original pirates in the light holding hands and smiling.

"It's time for me to leave and take my ship," said Zang. "They are waiting."

"You can't leave us here!" said Sally with tears in her eyes. "We haven't done anything really to help you."

"Oh, you have, my little friends. You showed the honor of friendship. You showed loyalty and love for one another. And you showed leadership. You have passed the test that the original pirates put in place many centuries ago. It began with the Pirates' Code of Trust, Honor, Loyalty, and Bravery, and you have shown that it is still alive and well in each of you. This is why you were brought here, remember—for the original pirates to see you and learn that I have done my job as the Guardian. Now it is time for me to pass that duty on to you. It is now your turn to be the Guardians."

"What! *Us* the *Guardians*?" quoted Joey as he shoved a Wonder Cake back into his pocket.

"Be brave, my mateys and lass. Share yourselves well. "Good-bye!" And with that last word, Zang boarded *The Black Widow*, took his place at the helm, and sailed into the light. The great and mighty ship, *The Black Widow*, carrying the souls of the original pirates along with their secrets was now free to float high in the sky carrying the pirates' spirits to the Pirate Star. When they arrived, all seven points shone brighter for all sailors to follow. We see it each night as the North Star.

"Do you think he will ever come back?" asked Sally?

With his hands behind his back, Joey said, "I don't know. But look what he left us!" Grinning, he held up the Pirates' Code Book. "He must have liked my Wonder Cakes, too. They're all gone!"

CHAPTER 22

JERRY AWOKE FIRST the next morning. Looking around, he saw no ship. Even the mud pit was gone—and the sun was shining. It was going to be a grand day. He covered the dying embers of their fire with earth and woke all his buddies.

"We'd better head back to town," he told them. "Our folks will be wondering where we've been!"

"I'm hungry," said Joey.

"The hike back to our bikes won't take too long," said Sam. "And the ride back is even shorter. Hey, Sally, is your mom working at the diner this morning? We can eat pancakes if she is."

"You know playing pirates and looking for golden eggs wore me out," said Cal as he squirmed out of his sleeping bag. I had the strangest dream last night! I dreamed I was a captain in the Royal Navy and my named was Thaddeus Greybellow!"

"After climbing in the caves and up and down those rocks," said Tom, "I slept like a log! But I do remember something about trying to get some guy named Zang back to the light, whatever that is!"

"I had a dream like that too!" said Sally. "Pretending to dress up like a lady from the 1700s wasn't easy, and some fool named Kilo tried to kill me! I think I made friends with you, Tom, but you weren't called Tom . . . you were Zang."

"Next time you want me to look through pirate books for stories with magic feathers and eggs," said Cal, "better ask Sally. She is better at puzzles than I am. She proved that in my dream when we were trying to figure one out."

At that instant, everyone looked at one another. It seemed they had all had the same dream . . . or had they?

"Oh, that's crazy!" said Jerry. "Let's go! We just told too many stories and ate too many Wonder Cakes last night. The next thing you'll be telling me is that we are Guardians now!"

Something unusual happened on that campout, thought Jerry as he looked at all his friends' faces. *We all became better friends, helped each other through our fears, and found trust in who we are.*

They hiked to their bikes then went riding down the trail away from the tree house. All the way, adventures of pirates swirled in their heads.

"Did anyone see the ship this morning?" questioned Joey.

"No, but I saw pirates floating in a bright light up to that stars last night," yelled Tom. "You know, the North Star!"

They continued to chatter and laugh as they rode. They shared their dreams and their recollections of their adventure at the campout. They finally decided it was the stories they told around the campfire the night before that had given them their dreams. But for some reason they all felt good about themselves and knew their friendship was worthwhile. They had helped each other through the trials of fear and brought their friendships closer than ever. It was going to be a good summer after all.

In town, they rode by the old oak tree, and there stood the old timer telling his stories to the town folks. Jerry stopped his bike to listen. The old timer looked him in the eye, smiled that crooked smile, and winked. "Remember mateys," he said. "What you think you see with your eyes isn't always what you really see!" Jerry rode down the street shaking his head, yelling, "Away with you, mateys!"

T HROUGHOUT MY LIFE I have told stories to my friends, family, co-workers, and relatives alike. I have written hundreds of short stories. For years, people have said to me, "Phyll, you should write books." So I did. I began this book on a plane when I was on my way to see my eldest son Kyle graduate from Navy boot camp. I wrote stories often on planes whenever I flew; it was a habit. Usually my stories were about some funny thing that had just happened to me. I wrote one because some people needed directions to my house (as odd as that sounds). I wrote a short story that contained the directions. My guests just laughed!

It took eleven years to write this book what with time out for work, illness, and who knows what else. But it has been a work of love, and I have found so much laughter and entertainment in writing it. I guess you could say that this book is for all those who thought I could not write, as well as for those who thought I should.

I have lived a life full of adventure, play, wonder, movies, and stories. I have always been amazed at what people will listen too. When I have told my stories, people's faces have just lit up when something struck their funny bone or evoked a personal memory. That above all brought joy to me. The pretend world is a place I go where I can find any adventure I want, and I never have to leave my front porch. To lie in the soft green clover at the neighborhood park and look up into the sky and picture all the wonders of the world is a playground within itself.

I sincerely hope that, no matter what age you are, you will allow your imagination to see the beautiful pictures and the endless stories that go with them throughout your life.

CPSIA information can be obtained at www.ICGtesting.com
Printed in the USA
BVOW03s1128230913

331896BV00006B/182/P